The Sloughhouse Letters

This book is a work of fiction. The characters, incidents, and dialogues are products of the author's imagination and are not to be construed as real. Any resemblance to actual persons, living or dead, or historical events is purely coincidental.

Printed by Kindle Direct Publishing, an Amazon.com Company. eStore address:
(www.kindle.com/Sloughhouse_Letters)

Available from Amazon.com, Kindle.com, and other retail bookstore outlets.

First printing September, 2021

Printed in the United States of America

Library of Congress Cataloging-in-Publication Data is on file with the publisher.

ISBN: 9798509542459
Imprint: Independently published

NOVELS BY DEL TRITTEN

The Last Mountain Man - *The Blackhammer Trilogy*

The Silent Battle of Dawn

The Return to Golden Mountain

The Fall from Rubicon Point

The Incan

Adolf's Gold - *A Nick Falkenrath Adventure*

The Delta Elite - *A Clifton Brakemeyer Mystery*

Lust & Lawsuits

Treasure of the Chancel Knights

Adolf's Ghost - *A Nick Falkenrath Adventure*

The Seven Sages of Apophis

Scrolls from the Wall of the Crow

Domus Mortis – *House of Death*

The Sloughouse Letters - *A Clifton Brakemeyer Mystery*

DEDICATION

For Mrs. Nancy Longnecker. My second favorite mom from my youth.

ACKNOWLEDGEMENTS

I would like to acknowledge my wife Caren for her patience and help wordsmithing this written work. I also acknowledge Carol Maynard for her outstanding skill in proofing the story architecture and prose. I wish to thank Pixabay.com for cover and interior images.

QUOTATIONS

It is impossible to suffer without making someone pay for it; every complaint already contains revenge.
Friedrich Nietzsche

If you lose a big fight, it will worry you all of your life. It will plague you - until you get your revenge.
Muhammad Ali

The alternate domination of one faction over another, sharpened by the spirit of revenge natural to party dissension, which in different ages and countries has perpetrated the most horrid enormities, is itself a frightful despotism. But this leads at length to a more formal and permanent despotism.
George Washington

If you prick us do we not bleed? If you tickle us do we not laugh? If you poison us do we not die? And if you wrong us shall we not revenge?
William Shakespeare

To write is a relief from life's problems. It is a way in which you revenge yourself. In art, the writer achieves utopia. But any attempt to achieve social utopia is bound to catastrophe. If you want a society of saints, the result is hell, repression, totalitarianism, and persecution.
Mario Vargas Llosa

AUTHOR'S NOTE

In the novel *The Delta Elite*, Clifton Brakemeyer fished the Sacramento Delta's Snodgrass Slough one warm summer morning. He snagged his line on something large and drifting. The fisherman dove in the murky slough and brought a trussed body to the surface.

The body was an old friend from high school, Johnny McCall. The retired Navy SEAL and San Francisco City Police Detective vowed to find Johnny's killer and bring him to justice.

Brakemeyer's former partner, Detective Calvin Chu, assisted his friend unofficially. Clif's investigation led him to Boston where the men he intended to question turned up dead.

Julia Delmar, the millionaire art patron and sponsor of Brakemeyer's investigation and art career, suddenly disappeared. The unofficial detective and artist known as Sam Lion narrowly escaped multiple assassination attempts.

As Brakemeyer closed in on the killer of Johnny McCall, he became a hostage of fanatics determined to solve earth's overpopulation problem. Julia Delmar and Detective Chu also became captives of the murderous group. Disease and killer insects threatened everyone. Brakemeyer had to survive and save his friends. He also had to face Johnny's killer, and stop the mad plans of the group calling themselves the *Defenders of Jasoom.*

The final fight between Johnny's killer, the Defenders of Jasoom, and Clifton Brakemeyer took place in the enormous manufacturing building between Cochrane Street and Hussey Street within the San Francisco Naval Shipyard, a Superfund Cleanup Site at Hunter's Point. Niles T. Ramey, the killer of Johnny McCall and many others, and the evil doctor that infected millions of biting insects with deadly diseases, met their doom. However, several key members of the *Defenders of Jasoom* escaped. The following story reveals their vengeance.

The #1 favorite of a select group of readers

The Sloughhouse Letters

A Clifton Brakemeyer Mystery

By

Del Tritten

One
The First & Second Letter

Ranjeet Bhabananda sat quietly in his prison cell at the California City Correctional Facility south-east of Bakersfield. His cellmate, a small Mexican gang member named Julio Huerta, lay on his bunk sketching the design of the tattoo he wanted to cover the last patch of unadorned skin remaining on his body – his right ass cheek.

Ranjeet's daily bag of mail from friends and family in Mumbai, India boosted his spirits. His correspondence allowed him to conduct gallery business at his Bhabananda Art Gallery, and communicate with his stockbroker who artfully kept the gallery owner's investments growing.

Convicted of manslaughter for the shooting death of Frederick Mahler, Ranjeet served only twenty-six months before having his conviction vacated. California prisons needed relief from overcrowding so releasing Ranjeet Bhabananda reduced prison congestion and filled an airline seat back to India. In one week, he would be a free man repatriated to his homeland.

The happy Hindi convict scooped up an odd-looking letter as his last bit of entertainment for the day. The number ten envelope, made of unusual tan parchment, featured his name, *care-of* prison address, and no sender information.

Ranjeet absently opened the envelope with a forefinger and extracted a second envelope. He opened it the same way and extracted a sheet of parchment paper. The chilling message brought a fear he'd not felt in years.

Nattukottai Chettiar Ranjeet Bhabananda:

The fact that you are reading this letter means you are a dead man. You killed Frederick Mahler out of malice and revenge. Your loyalty pledge to the group meant nothing to you. Now you will pay for your treachery. May Yama (Lord of Death) escort you through all 28 Narakas (hells) and leave you for all eternity in the very worst of them. Suspended on pitchforks and torn apart by ravenous dogs is my favorite. I wish that for you.

"Appear weak when you are strong and strong when you are weak."

Sun Tzu

Sweat beaded on the Hindi's forehead and a strange nausea crept upward from his bowels to his throat. Ranjeet studied the sheet and envelope. He detected a film made up of a talc-like powder. He smelled the tips of his fingers and the inside of the envelope. He thought he detected the slight bitter smell of almonds – cyanide.

His title of *Nattukottai Chettiar,* a title only known by a few people outside of India, and the reference of loyalty pledge to the group, meant the letter's progenitor originated within the *Defenders of Jasoom.*

The panicked Hindi stood and stumbled to his cell door. He yelled for help from a guard; no guard existed within earshot of the dying man.

"Help me! Help me someone! Guards help me, I've been poisoned."

Julio sat upright on his bunk. "Poisoned?" he asked. "How did you get poisoned?"

Ranjeet began to twitch and jerk. Foam leaked from his lips as he crashed to the floor writhing in spasmodic contractions.

"Don't . . . touch . . . the letter . . . Defenders of . . . Jasoom."

The poison victim lapsed into horrible squeaks, moans, and cries of pain. Julio stood and stepped to the door making certain to avoid touching his writhing cellmate.

"Guards! Guards! This *luces idiotas* is dying!"

Julio yelled for a good fifteen minutes when a guard strolled by and stopped to check out the ruckus.

"What's going on Huerta?" the guard yelled at Julio.

"Sir," the Mexican illegal replied. "This Cabrón got sick and fell! I think he's dying or dead."

The guard called for backup and the prison doctor. When they arrived, the doctor made a quick check of the dead man, queried Julio of what he heard and saw, and then quarantined the cell under HAZMAT regulations. The poison letter and all of Ranjeet's mail found their way into sealable containers by men in HAZMAT suits and respirators. The prison warden reviewed all the preliminary facts of the situation and knew he had a bureaucratic nightmare on his hands.

***

The Sacramento Delta's wintertime air bore crisp cerulean skies, a few wispy cirrus clouds, and a gentle breeze from the west. Clifton Brakemeyer's live-aboard yacht, the Lujon, floated quietly alongside the long dock at Willow Berm Marina & Yacht Harbor. Willow Berm clung to life a short quarter mile from the confluence of the Mokelumne River and San Joáquin River in the Sacramento Delta. The marina occupied half of the Mokelumne's width; it offered the best delta location for the Lujon's six feet of draft and 97 feet of floating luxury.

The Lujon's owner and self-proclaimed *delta river rat*, bundled in a sweater and new Levis, lounged on the chaise in front of the flybridge cabin. Brakemeyer sipped at a cup of rich, dark Columbian coffee and watched the occasional fishermen cruise up and down the river hunting for the most advantageous fishing spot radar could provide.

A curvaceous, black-haired beauty with doe-like brown eyes eased herself to a sitting position alongside her significant other. She sipped her coffee laced with crème and sugar and signed heavily.

Clif said, "That sigh sounded like a prelude to bad news. Care to explain?"

Gabrielle Uhlmann ran her index finger around the rim of her coffee mug. "You are too damn good at reading my mind and discerning my moods."

"Is it because your time with me has run out and you must return to Geneva?"

"No."

"Is it because I have been replaced in your heart by a dashing Swiss banker from Bern?"

"No."

"Is it because I don't visit you often enough leaving you unwilling to continue our long-distance relationship?"

Gaby fell silent focusing her vision on a heron pecking at edible objects in the shallows of the river. She breathed another sigh and sipped her rapidly cooling coffee.

"Alright," Clif said. "Out with it. Your intractableness is killing our happy visit, or do you prefer me to continue with twenty questions?"

"No."

Clif took his turn to play the silence gambit. First person to speak loses he thought.

After several long minutes, Gaby finally relented and said, "I'm pregnant."

A tear leaked from her eye, and then two. Suddenly a torrent of tears caused her to spill her coffee and dash for the big sectional sofa in the main cabin. Cliff counted to fifty," and then followed her inside the yacht. He walked to the galley and watched the weeping maiden. Refilling his near-empty coffee mug, the private detective quietly stepped to the sofa, sat next to his lady, and put his muscular arm around her shoulders.

Clif said, "To me your news sounds terrific. I'd love for you to quite Swiss Air, give notice on your apartment, and then move in with me. I am really excited at the prospects."

"I knew you'd say that," Gaby said almost choking on the words.

"Well of course," Clif replied. "What else should I say?"

The Swiss Air flight attendant pursed her lips and then shouted, "I don't want to raise my child on a boat amidst all this flat land and muddy water. Why can't you sell the Lujon and move to Switzerland with me? We can find a chalet with green pastures, lake, and mountain views. Our child's life would be so much richer and happier."

"You've never said a word to me about not liking my lifestyle or my work," Clif said. "I love Switzerland, but leaving my home and all I've come to love is a little scary, you know?"

"Me moving here is a lot scarier," Gaby barked. "Please take me to the airport. I wish to go home."

The tearful fräulein hustled to the master stateroom, threw her clothes into her overnight carry-on luggage bag, and then marched passed Brakemeyer and off the yacht.

Clif knew his lady well enough to know arguing would gain nothing. Discussion would gain nothing. He recognized her set jaw, squinty eyes, and tight lips as signs of an intractable will; a decision made and set in stone.

Dreading the long, silent drive to the San Francisco Airport, Clif retrieved his Corvette keys from the jewelry drawer in his dresser, and then headed for his car. His phone alerted him to a caller seeking an audience. Calvin Chu's name filled the small screen.

"Hello, Brakemeyer here."

"Clif, this is Cal. I just received a call from Beverly Wells. She tried to reach you but didn't have your new number. Anyway, she read where a member of the Defenders of Jasoom died in prison."

"So what? Happens all the time."

"No, you don't understand. It was Ranjeet Bhabananda, the man that shot Frederick Mahler."

"Again, I say so what? Scratch one lunatic and move on. What has Beverly so nervous she called you and me?"

"After reading about the unusual death of the Hindi art gallery owner, she used her press credentials to bully through the PR roadblocks at the San Bernardino County Coroner's Office. The preliminary toxicology report indicated Bhabananda died from a really toxic mixture of cyanide, ricin, and batrachotoxin probably from the poison arrow frog – very deadly, very, very deadly."

"How did that combination of poisons make its way into a state prison to kill an inmate?"

"Apparently a letter carried the poisons," Cal said. "As soon as he opened it, he touched and breathed in a deadly powder. He died in minutes. The funny thing is, according to Beverly, the man's manslaughter sentence was vacated. His release lay only days away."

"This is all very interesting, my friend, but I have a bit of a domestic crisis happening right now. I'm driving Gaby to the airport. We should talk about this later."

"No, no you don't understand," Cal pleaded.

"What the hell don't I understand?"

"Beverly coaxed the coroner into emailing her photos of the letter and envelope."

"Get to the point man! I've got a pissed-off Swiss lady getting angrier by the minute."

Cal shouted, "Beverly received a letter today matching the one that killed Bhabananda!"

"Oh shit," Cliff mumbled. "Phone Beverly, and let her know we are coming. I'll meet you at her place in three hours. Put the letter in an airtight container. Make certain you wear hazmat gloves, mask, and suit. Tell her to keep far from the letter and wash her hands thoroughly in case she touched the envelope. Have Johnson put a team together for blanket protection twenty-four-seven."

"Got it. See you in three."

Gaby stared up at Brakemeyer as he put away his phone and climbed down into the cockpit of his ZR1. As he settled in and roared the engine to life, Gaby brought her frosty stare to bare on Brakemeyer.

"So, you will drop me at Swiss Air and then run off to meet some woman named *Beverly*. Is that the same Beverly you visited in the Kantonsspital Uri in Altdorf? The same Beverly that accompanied you back to San Francisco?"

Clif wanted to fire back a response that would crush Gaby's petty attempt to instigate a fight. Instead, he calmed himself hoping to direct his girlfriend toward a civil discussion of their future together. He directed his Vette north on Brannon Island Road to Road 12 east to I-5 Interstate to 580 west.

After a very long and uncomfortable silence Clif said, "Beverly played an integral part in my murder investigation surrounding Gordon Wicks. Now it would appear the same person or persons that killed a member of the gang called the Defenders of Jasoom are threatening her life. Don't you remember? I told you the whole story that night we got drunk at McSorley's Pub and Steak House on the Arve River in Geneva."

Gaby folded her arms and stared silently through the side window. Clif decided he'd had enough of her temper. He might as well push her to the edge.

"It would appear my darling, that the only appeasement acceptable to you is my agreement to totally uproot my life and my business and move to Switzerland. I am sorry if I am not prepared at this moment to agree to such a momentous realignment. With all the time we spent apart over the last two years, how do I know that *'a'* you are truly pregnant, *'b'* if you are truly pregnant that the baby is mine, or *'c'* you are proffering a cruel way to break up with me? Why are you suddenly pregnant after two years of a long-distance relationship?"

Brakemeyer thought for a moment Gaby would jump out of the car or perhaps fish a weapon out of her purse and use it on him. He drew glances at her while keeping the majority of his attention on the road.

"You are a cruel bastard," Gaby yelled through choking sobs. "I'm pregnant precisely because it's been two years!"

Clif failed to grasp her logic. He said, "I do not care if you are pregnant. In fact, I love the fact that you are pregnant. What I am trying to understand is why you are not willing to live with me among the palm trees and waters of the delta. I grew up here and believe me it is not a bad life. Our baby would grow up with all the advantages of living rural."

"Oh, so now it's *our baby*," Gaby cried. "Maybe our baby belongs to a Swiss Air pilot or a guy I picked up in a bar, or an old boyfriend?"

"Look Gabs, I love you and no one else," Clif replied. "I want you and our baby to be together, here with me in this wonderful place. Hell, there is world class skiing, snowboarding, and sledding just two and a half hours away. The Redwoods and Pacific Ocean are a half-day drive to the west, San Francisco, Santa Cruz, Monterey are there to visit anytime. Lake Tahoe and the Sierra Mountains to the east are wondrous."

Gaby maintained a code of silence on the remaining drive to the San Francisco Airport. At the curbside drop off for Swiss Air, Clif attempted to give his love a hug and kiss, but she pushed him away. Head held high and proud, she marched stiff-legged into the terminal and out of his life.

***

Brakemeyer walked into Beverly Wells' apartment to find a sealed container by the front door with Cal and Bev yakking it up on the couch, drinks in hand.

"I hope you took photos of the envelope before sealing it in the container," Clif said. "We need to compare it to the photos of the envelope that killed the Hindi art dealer."

"Bev sent them to my cellphone before I snapped a few images of her envelope," Cal answered. "To me, the envelopes appear to be of the same parchment paper and computer typesetting. We should take it to the warehouse in Reno for examination."

"My thoughts also," Clif said. He sat down on the sofa and asked, "Beverly, do you still have the letter Julia Delmar sent you detailing the Defenders of Jasoom? We should make a list of all people connected with the Gordon Wicks case. One column will show those that died and one that shows those who did not die."

Beverly excused herself. She returned from her bedroom office with the letter sent to her by Julia Delmar. Brakemeyer pulled a writing tablet and pencil from his man-bag.

He said, "The left column represents those persons connected to the Gordon Wicks case that are known to be dead:

1. Frederick Mahler
2. Julia Broderick Delmar
3. Roberto Spawn
4. Niles T. Ramey
5. Professor Louis D'Arceau
6. Avery McMichaels
7. Derrick Pullman
8. Dr. Helmut Mueller
9. Ranjeet Bhabananda (he killed Frederick Mahler)

Ranjeet Bhabananda represents the last death after a two-year hiatus of murder and mayhem. We know that Niles Ramey, Roberto Spawn, and Willie Poe took care of the group's wet work as directed by Frederick Mahler and Acucena Cascalho. As leader of the Defenders of Jasoom, Mahler decided to eliminate those members of his organization that rebelled or refused to accompany him on his road to madness and death of billions. Therefore, our right-side column represents those persons connected to the Wicks case that are still alive:

1. Gordon Wicks (prison)
2. Acucena Cascalho (personal assistant to Frederick Mahler)
3. Willie Poe (assassin)
4. Mary Ellis Martin (art history professor UC Berkeley)
5. Sheldon A. Bathingswait (retired director Del Morton living in Portugal.)
6. Marcel Karelle (art gallery owner Brussels)
7. Nashwa Zahur (art gallery owner South Africa)
8. Bao-Yu Ming (art gallery owner Taiwan)
9. Beverly Wells (ARTnews magazine journalist)

10. Robert Blevins (CEO Global International)
11. Calvin Chu (retired S.F. Police Detective)
12. Clifton Brakemeyer (retired Navy SEAL, retired S.F. Police Detective, owner B-Delta Security.)"

Beverly spoke with a sour taste in her mouth. "All twelve people are on the hit parade of murder."

"The killer is likely to be one in the group," Cal said.

"I think we can eliminate you, me, and Beverly," Clif said. "That leaves nine. Which one has an axe to grind?"

"You sent Wicks to jail," Cal remarked. "If he killed the Hindi with a poison letter, how did he manage that from prison?"

"Wicks' motive is strong," Clif mused.

"Acucena Cascalho served Mahler as personal assistant and Treasurer of the Defenders of Jasoom," Beverly added. "If she loved Mahler, maybe she is trying to avenge his death. Nevertheless, why kill all of us? She can't be benefitted in any way except for some juvenile sense of revenge."

"She represented the total fanatic package of an insane environmentalist," Clif said. "Her conviction that the earth's human population had to be culled to a sustainable level scared the crap out of me. I felt like I was gazing at Mephistopheles in drag. Wicks and Cascalho share no common traits."

"Except for revenge," Beverly said.

UNITED STATES POST OFFICE
SLOUGHHOUSE CALIFORNIA 95683

Two

The Second & Third Letters

Clif Brakemeyer owned the Reno warehouse under the business name of Sam Lion, LLC IBC (International Business Company) based in the Cayman Islands. The 20,000 square foot box supported the work of B-DELTA Security, an international private security, risk management, and defense contracting company. The city of Reno, County of Washoe, and State of Nevada believed the warehouse served inventory storage purposes.

Clif owned 80% of the business and Cal owned 20%. Clif, Cal, and their security team all received taxable pay from the Sam Lion Cayman LLC dba B-DELTA Security. Profits, however, grew nicely in secure, non-taxable investments handled by a broker in Georgetown, the Cayman Islands capital.

The warehouse contained an emergency medical facility, chemical lab, and computer center. Clif and Cal brought the sealed container into the building and straight to the chemical lab. The single paid employee, Dr. Henry Sellers, took care of all the Security team's medical and chemical problems. As a retired Navy medical officer, Henry double dipped by receiving his Navy retirement and a handsome salary from B-DELTA Security.

"Hank," Clif said, "this sealed container may carry an envelope and letter laced with cyanide, ricin, and batrachotoxin. I need you to set up a clean room that will contain toxins, and then examine the envelope. If it is dirty, seal it in the container. An incinerator will destroy the problem."

"I assume you want a photo inventory of the envelope and letter regardless of poisons?" Hank asked.

"As soon as possible," Cal added. "We may have a letter assassin working overtime. *Yours truly* is on the list of targets."

Brakemeyer and Chu spent the afternoon in the computer center chasing leads on creating homemade poisons, and building a list of addresses and phone numbers for the names on the living side of the Wicks case ledger. The possibility existed that letters would soon reach those people. A proactive approach may save their lives, even if they didn't deserve it. They decided to ask Beverly to contact the eight names on the *living* list to warn them of pending trouble.

At 5:30 p.m., Hank remained sequestered in his makeshift clean room. Clif and Cal decided to break for dinner at the spectacular Bimini Steakhouse in the Peppermill Casino. *Stunning* best described the huge room lighted with blue recessed lights, red curtains, and backlit images of the world's most spectacular scenery.

Clif's phone buzzed. "What's up Hank? Yeah . . . yeah . . . anything else? Send me a photo of the letter ASAP. Okay, thanks Hank."

"What's the word," Cal mumbled through bites of a delicious beef tenderloin fillet.

"No poisons in, on, or around the letter," Clif replied. "Not a trace of anything nasty other than a partial fingerprint from a dirty finger. Hank is sending me photos of the letter and envelope. He'll run the partial fingerprint through the FBI's Integrated AFIS system. I asked him to use Photoshop to mirror the print into a full finger version that might reveal a person if the partial does not."

Clif's phone alerted him to an incoming text message. He checked it to examine the photos of the letter and envelope. Clif examined the photos and then handed the phone to Cal.

"I want to return to the warehouse and open Beverly's photos and these photos on the big, dual computer screens for a better examination."

Cal nodded and scarfed the remainder of his excellent steak dinner.

***

The two men sat side by side examining every part of the two different images of the letters. The first job to perform involved the letter and message for Beverly Wells. Her letter read as follows:

Beverly Carol Wells

ARTnews Magazine

If you are reading this letter, you will soon be dead. Your complicity with Julia Delmar destroyed the work that would have saved planet earth. Your journalistic fervor and cooperation with the police and Sam Lion are reason enough to end your days.

All war is deception.

Sun Tzu

"Interesting that the assassins used my artist moniker instead of my real name," Clif remarked. "Instead of the statement of death as in the Bhabananda letter, Beverly received a warning or threat of death."

"Why not use poison on Beverly as they did with Ranjeet Bhabananda?" Cal queried. "Why give her the opportunity to protect herself? This doesn't make sense."

"Never commit murder the same way twice," Clif stated. "How many different ways is there to kill someone without kidnapping."

"Why no kidnapping?" Cal asked.

"I'm not certain, but the assassins appear to be hands off. They kill with poison letters; we know that. They could shoot her sniper style."

"Or sneak a poisonous snake or spider in her apartment."

"Or explode a bomb in her car."

"They could sneak poison into her food or drink in a public restaurant or bar."

Clif pushed his face closer to the computer monitor. "Cal, look at the postmark on the envelope sent to the Hindi art dealer. It's difficult to make out the words as they blur across the stamp. Now look at the postmark on Beverly's envelope. The postmark clearly reads *Sloughhouse*. I'll blow up the section of the Bhabananda envelope image where the postmark covers the stamp."

Cal said, "Looks to me like it says Sloughhouse. What the hell? Why would someone go to all the trouble to send poison letters and hate mail from a nowhere burg between Sacramento and Rancho Murieta?"

"The sender isn't being random about these letters or how they are mailed," Clif said. "The style of the communique, the specific words, the Sun Tzu quotes, and the postmarks from Sloughhouse all mean something."

"Like what?"

"Like I have no idea. We need to open communications with each of the nine *alive* people on our list to see if any of them receive or received a letter."

"I believe I should work closely with Beverly on this," Cal said nonchalantly.

Clif smiled and gave Cal a knowing glance. "Oh, *duplicitous* is thy middle name. What happened to your *significant other* Doctor May Tockterman?"

"We have uncoupled as they say," Cal responded. "I'll tell you the story some other time. Besides, working with Beverly is business, strictly business."

"Beverly being smart, beautiful, and available has nothing whatever to do with anything, right?" Clif laughed.

"I thought Phil Baldwin laid claim to the art journalist?" Cal asked.

"Beverly prefers men with an edge of danger to their personalities. Phil Baldwin's selfhood aligns more closely with Napoleon Dynamite."

***

Brakemeyer felt better knowing Cal watched over Beverly. With B-DELTA Security people on the job also, Clif knew he could concentrate on heading off the next victim.

After returning to the Lujon from the Reno warehouse, Clif phoned Robert Blevins, CEO of Global International and warned him of the letter assassin. Blevins promised to be on the lookout for a parchment letter with no return address and a postmark of Sloughhouse.

After the demolition of Frederick Mahler's death factories, the members of the Defenders of Jasoom fled to their respective countries prepping their attorneys to fight extradition. When Brakemeyer breached their defenses of call-screeners, blocked cell phone numbers, and attorneys, the targets for murder expressed thanks and an unspoken level of understanding.

Brakemeyer knew contacting the eight remaining targets meant alerting the letter assassin to his investigative presence. Perhaps he could draw out the assassin by focusing the killer's efforts on Sam Lion.

Clif's last contact would be the man he disliked the most, Gordon Wicks. The former elite delta rancher received a sentence of consecutive ten-year prison terms for theft, conspiracy, extortion, and accomplice to felony murder.

The owner of B-DELTA Security decided to drive the six hours of I-5 south to the Terminal Island Federal Prison in Los Angeles Harbor. Due to Wicks' advanced age a Federal Judge moved him to Terminal Island better known as Club Fed. Its minimum-security designation meant less dangerous criminals inhabited the rectangular peninsula protruding into Los Angeles Harbor.

Surrounded by seawater and a Coast Guard Base, the Federal Correctional Institution offered prisoners Advanced Occupational Education. They received apprenticeships, library services, a UNICOR facility for producing furniture and industrial products, and Commissary where the prison's one thousand inmates could spend $400 per month.

Gordon Wicks delved deep into the available art activities including paintings and sketches in oils, pastels, plus pen and ink. The man fancied himself an excellent artist producing clay and wood sculptures, paintings in oil using the Bob Ross wet-on-wet technique, and charcoal sketches consisting of his ranch memories with tractors, levees, and date palms.

The prisoner visitation center, a large room divided by long rows of tables, allowed friends and family to sit across from their loved ones. Only a sheet of clear plastic separated visitors from inmates.

"I wondered when you'd get around to paying me a visit Brakemeyer," Gordon Wicks said casually.

"You know why I am here you smug, pretentious, pompous ass," Brakemeyer replied. "You don't deserve to live out your time in Club Fed."

"Not only that," Wicks said. "I've made over $2,000 from my paintings and sculptures. My broker has found dealers and gallery owners that love prison artwork. Consumers seem fascinated by the creative criminal mind."

"Have you received a letter threatening your life?"

"Not yet," Wicks said. "Will I receive one? What is going on in your world, Brakemeyer?"

The private detective studied Wicks' face for deceit. He knew the man to be capable of larceny while denying involvement completely, and with a straight face.

"You probably already know this, but Ranjeet Bhabananda died after handling a poison-laced letter in his jail cell. A judge vacated his sentence. He died three days before being released to return to India."

"Now there's a bit of bad luck," Wicks said smiling. "What would that have to do with me?"

"I'm sure you remember Beverly Wells, yes?"

"Yes, of course. Julia spoke of her often."

"Beverly received an identical letter threatening her life."

Brakemeyer watched Wicks' eyes for a hint that he would know her letter contained no poisons. Wicks, however, maintained a blank stare that revealed nothing.

"So, did she die of poisoning also?" the happy prisoner asked.

"You are the prick of all time," Clif said in a low, menacing voice. "My only regret is I didn't club you half to death with an orchard pole when I had the chance."

"If someone is out to kill the remaining maniacs in the Defenders of Jasoom that is not my problem. Julia told me about the group but I never took part in their operations. In fact, I fell victim to their operations when they killed my guard and stole my antiquities. You know that."

"Your fake antiquities," Brakemeyer said. "I don't suppose you'd contact me if you receive one of these assassination letters?"

J. Gordon Wicks stood and straightened his white prison pants and shirt. He said, "We are done with our little chat Mr. Sam Lion. Leave me your contact phone number. I will call you should I receive one of these letters. Do they have a particular look or commonality?"

"Number ten envelope, parchment stock, and computer typewritten text signed with a Sun Tzu quote. If I find that you are the instigator of these revenge killings, I shall find a friend within the walls of this facility that will pay you a one-time visit. I am finding a new career metering out justice to killers who've avoided it."

The smile fell from Wicks' face. He said, "My next call will be to my attorney relating your death threat Brakemeyer. You always were a cocky kid with more brass than brains."

Brakemeyer broke out his own smile. "I put your snarky ass in jail, didn't I?"

***

On the return drive from San Pedro to Willow Berm, Brakemeyer took a hands-free call in his Corvette. Robert Blevins sounded breathless and overwrought.

"Mr. Brakemeyer," Blevins said, "I just received a letter that matches the description you gave me of the letters sent to the prisoner that died and to Beverly Wells."

"I am returning from Los Angeles and am about an hour away from you. I will bring a sealable container. Do not touch the letter. In fact, stay as far from it as possible. Just because Beverly's letter contained no poisons does not mean yours won't kill you in some fashion. I'll take it to my lab, analyze it, and then suggest a course of action for you. In the meantime, I will assign two of my security agents to watch you around the clock."

After stopping at an office supply store in San Mateo, Clif parked in his usual spot under the Pyramid Building and made his way up to Blevins' office. By the time he reached the 40th floor, blue latex gloves covered his hands, a white jump suit covered his body and head, and a three-ply surgical mask covered the breathing parts of his face.

"Should we contact the police?" Robert Blevins asked.

"We have the right to examine suspect mail," Clif said. "The San Francisco City Police have been alerted to the letter received by Beverly Wells. Cal or I will advise them of this letter once we have placed it under the microscope. In the meantime, a team of my security agents will cover you around the clock."

"What's that going to cost?" Blevins complained.

"Much less than the cost of your life."

***

By the time Clif reached the Reno warehouse at midnight, his muscles and bones felt the ordeal of his sports car junket. The road warrior contemplated trading in his Corvette for a Lincoln MKZ.

Henry Sellers' day started at 8:00 a.m. leaving Clif the opportunity to catch some shut-eye on a hospital bed in the medical unit of the warehouse.

When the doctor arrived, he pulled his car into the warehouse through a rollup door on the east end of the big concrete block. He parked alongside Clif's Corvette and knew something was *afoot* for the boss to be here already.

The clean room remained intact so after a cup of strong coffee and some discussion, Hank sequestered himself and began his analysis of the Blevins letter. Clif retired to the computer room to enter the details of his Gordon Wicks visit on his networked thinking machine. The computers in the warehouse, Lujon, Delta Junk, and the B-DELTA Security Training Facility networked together and shared data. The one person the computer did not link to - Gabrielle Uhlmann, and he hadn't heard from her in days.

Hank strolled into the computer room. "No fingerprints, poisons, or contaminants of any kind. Care to check out the letter?"

"No need," Brakemeyer said. "Send your photos to me so I may compare and contrast with the other two letters."

In moments, the images arrived. Clif read the text:

Global International, Inc.

Mr. Robert Blevins, CEO

Death by a thousand cuts will consume Global International, Inc. and you can do nothing to stop it. Your stock will plummet; your life will crash. Redemption is impossible. The traitor Julia Delmar and her company will receive justice posthumously.

If you know the enemy and know yourself, you need not fear the results of a hundred battles.

Sun Tzu

Brakemeyer split his two computer screens by placing the first two letter images on the left side monitor and the third letter on the right. The death threat though different, remained the key to each letter's purpose. Letter to Bhabananda – you are already dead. The letter to Beverly – you will soon be dead. The letter to Bob Blevins – death by a thousand cuts – your life will soon crash. Postmark on all three letters – Sloughhouse.

Three
The Third & Fourth Letters

The man standing on the eastside walk, in the center of the Golden Gate Bridge, calmly held a small actuator in his right hand. Its range extended to a quarter mile. He wore a cheap, light gray sweat suit with a thick white towel wrapped around his neck. Sunglasses and a thick mustache disguised his face. His long brown hair hung straight down his back, held to a ponytail at the base of his neck with a rubber band.

The noonday sun consumed the a.m. fog, creating a sparkling, crisp winter's day. A brisk breeze brought whitecaps to blue bay waters.

Beginning as a speck on the horizon, the world's third largest container vessel, the MGS Achelois grew larger in its approach to the bay. The pretend jogger waited until a group of bicycling tourists passed him on their way to Sausalito, and the vessel passed beneath the bridge. As its stern became entirely visible, he pressed the actuator button.

The simultaneous explosions inside four shipping containers sent a blue flash of light streaking out from between the vessel's cargo. A shudder ripped through the ship knocking many seamen off their feet. Luckily, the blasts occurred with nine containers on each side, three containers below, five containers front and back, and four containers on top. Had the affected containers been stacked last, the detonation would have opened them up like a sunrise opening a morning glory.

Observing black smoke billowing from the aft container group, the captain sounded the emergency alarm. The deep klaxon blast resembled a tuba hitting low C. It echoed over the waters warning craft to steer and tack clear of the ship's troubled path. The container vessel Achelois continued to cry and wallow through the choppy bay waters to the Oakland International Container Terminal.

The captain and helmsman followed the instructions of the port authority. They guided the huge vessel to the turning basin in the Oakland Outer

Harbor Channel. The captain constantly updated his ship's status to the port authorities at the Ports America Outer Harbor Terminal.

Two fireboats arrived and began cannonading seawater onto the smoking containers. As the smoke subsided, tugboats carefully nudged the huge vessel toward its berth in the quay. Soon after, City of Oakland Police arrived and stood about shooing away the curious. Fire trucks, paramedics, an ISC Alameda Coast Guard rescue team, the Alameda County Bomb Squad, and port authority safety inspectors waited for the Achelois to dock.

The plan the experts concocted involved the evacuation of all ship's personnel, the offloading of the shifted containers surrounding the exploded ones, and the perilous inspection of the damaged area. Following these procedures, the four blown containers would find sequestration on the B25-26 section of the quay yard for further forensic analysis.

Eight hours passed and night arrived before the gantry cranes lifted the Global International, Inc. containers off the ship. The shredded steel boxes found themselves wrapped in special steel straps and lifted off the vessel and onto the quay yard. A straddle carrier lifted them and slowly rolled them to their predetermined locations.

After teams of inspectors and bomb experts carefully used their high-tech equipment to thoroughly search, scan, and photograph the wreckage, the bomb-sniffing dogs set to work hunting for explosive remnants.

***

Based upon the Oakland port authority's phone call, his containers exploded at 10 a.m. yesterday. Upon learning the scope of the terrorist attack on his shipment of furniture, home decorations, and appliances, CEO Blevins immediately called Lloyds of London. He anticipated that his insurance would cover the loss of the items in the shipment.

However, this disaster would leave his west coast retail locations and his online warehouses short of inventory. He would soon have insurance agents crawling all over his business. His insurance rates would skyrocket. Even Lloyds would not accept a client targeted by incendiaries without extracting exorbitant premiums.

His buyers in Asia would have to scramble to purchase replacements for the inventory and hire dependable protection to assure the shipping containers were not booby-trapped. Costs would soar.

If this was one cut out of a thousand, the company was doomed. Blevins remembered every word of the letter. The image sent by his corporate troubleshooter placed his company and his life in jeopardy. He reasoned that if the perpetrators of this crime sought some crazy kind of revenge against Global's former owner, Julia Delmar, the company and his life would fall into permanent disrepair.

The letter mentioned *the traitor* Julia Delmar, his former boss. She founded Global International, Inc. and built it into a retail empire until her sudden death at the hands of art thieves – of which she was a part. He knew so little of her tragic demise, and her private life, that her inclusion in this letter made little sense. Wasn't her death enough for these maniacs?

Blevins called the police and informed them of the letter. A detective, Karl, arrived at his office on the 40th floor of the Pyramid Building in San Francisco. He grilled Robert Blevins as though the CEO knew everything about Julia Delmar, her associates, and Clifton Brakemeyer. Blevins repeated what everyone that followed the news knew of those three people. Karl drilled Blevins on Julia Delmar's art world associates of which he knew almost nothing. The detective snapped the CEO's last nerve.

"Damn it Detective Karl," Blevins shouted. "I met Julia's fancy-pants art crowd only once. I said hello to the delta rancher Gordon Wicks, Frederick Mahler the art gallery big shot, and Clifton Brakemeyer. I shook the hands of a dozen people with forgettable names and faces. Julia sucked the former detective into investigating the murder at the Wick's Ranch by promising to make Brakemeyer a successful artist. Well, he's a better investigator than he is an artist. In the end, Julia followed her son into the afterlife, and Brakemeyer's partner, Calvin Chu, contracted the AIDS virus. Brakemeyer recovered some antiquities that Wicks stole and then claimed a reward in the millions of dollars. Moreover, Julia gifted him her yacht in exchange for a bunch of his paintings. The detective turned artist turned investigator is this company's troubleshooter. He is, in fact, my next phone call."

Detective Karl said, "Thank you for your help, Mr. Blevins – I think. At least I know what my next call will be."

Blevins punched the auto-dial number for Clif Brakemeyer.

"Mr. Brakemeyer," Blevins said, "would you tell me why Julia is referred to as a traitor by these terrorists? What did she do that left me this awful legacy? What did she do that created so much hate?"

Clif tried to avoid the subject but knew his client had a right to know. "Do you remember Julia's son?" he asked.

"Yes – an artist wanna be as I recall. His name was Aaron I think."

"Aaron's gay lifestyle brought him into contact with Niles T. Ramey and Willie Poe. They, in turn, brought him into contact with Acucena Cascalho. She turned him into a zero-population fanatic. He pulled his mother and her money into a secret group called the Defenders of Jasoom. They were composed of art gallery owners, dealers, distributors, and museum curators. They swindled money from collectors, museums, and non-affiliated galleries. All the money went toward building a world-wide network of insect breeding facilities designed to spread disease to the poorest populations around the world."

Blevins interrupted and asked, "How did Julia get on their bad side?"

"The group's front included donations to *zero population groups* working to save the planet with zero population propaganda. That is what Julia thought she supported. When she found out the group paid killers to remove anyone posing a danger to the group, she sent a letter to Beverly Wells. The letter outlined all the people involved and their dirty deeds. By accident I became involved with Beverly throwing me head first into the group's crazy plan."

"I understand Aaron died at some point," Blevins said.

"His boyfriend, Niles Ramey, found out Aaron had AIDS and very likely infected Niles. Julia took her son to Mexico where he underwent treatments for the disease not available in the U.S. While there,

Niles tracked him down and killed him making it look like an accident. Eventually, Ramey and Poe captured Julia where she became a test guinea pig for the scientist employed by the group to infect the insects."

"Did she die from a disease given her during testing?" Blevins asked.

"No," Clif said sadly. "They threw her and Calvin Chu naked into one of the trailers. They pumped in infected mosquitos and tsetse flies. I saved Cal but Julia was too far-gone. Her mind broke under the horror of their torture."

"Oh my god," Blevins said. "Those rotten bastards. Do you think someone from the group is behind these killings and bombings?"

Clif said, "It certainly is possible. Cal and I are investigating."

Robert Blevins spoke in a low tone voice laced with menace. "I'll pay you every last nickel of this company's coffers plus my own money to catch the person behind this evil. God speed Mr. Brakemeyer."

***

"God, I miss Commander Marcs," Brakemeyer said somberly. "Johnson is a brave agent, but not the knowledgeable organizer and leader that Marcs was."

Cal thought a moment and then said to his partner, "I have reviewed dozens of résumés, and interviewed dozens of potential candidates. I have not found that combination of experience, command under fire, and background free of baggage."

I know someone that is more qualified than the late Commander Marcs. She's recently retired from the German BND. I considered contacting her ever since my trip to Europe."

"Really," Cal said in mild astonishment. "How do we employ this wunderkind?"

"Well, that's the tricky part," Brakemeyer replied. "She is the girlfriend or significant other of one of our clients. You met him at Marc's funeral – Nick Falkenrath. I would have to persuade him as well as her to agree to her temporary employment. That won't be easy."

Cal gave his friend and collaborate a sinister glance. He said, "You didn't by chance meet up with this BND Colonel after you accompanied Gaby back to Switzerland? You hung around a few days after she returned to work at Swiss Air."

Clif said, "I have no response to that."

Cal smiled and asked, "How were things in Sokolov, Czechia, and Germany? I read where Marc's killer, a Nuevo-Nazi named Herta Hildegund, was assassinated by a long-range sniper."

Brakemeyer's poker face revealed nothing. He said, "I think the Russians did it. All I know is that retired Colonel Ada Schmidt is sharp and knows what she is doing, and could help us immeasurably."

"Gaby is not going to be crazy about your working closely with another woman agent especially a German," Cal said. "Why did Gaby leave early to return home? You indicated during our phone conversation that an angry Swiss lady neared an implosion. What happened?"

Clif sighed and said, "I don't want to discuss my difficulties with Gaby. I'll consult you for a solution when we solve this case."

Cal said, "Don't play the stoic silent man carrying his burdens alone in a world of trouble. Don't forget I'm your friend as well as your partner. By the way, how is your ex-wife's law suit against you coming along?"

Clif shrugged and said, "Susan sued me for assault, battery, malicious intent to drown, and the ruin of her very expensive Gucci dress and handbag - $500,000 in round numbers. I offered to pay for the dress and bag and ten-grand for her pain and suffering. It was worth that much but not any additional. The battle between lawyers rages on. They will be the big winners."

"Gaby Uhlmann is a saint. I hope you don't lose her my friend," Cal said. "You even talked about moving to Switzerland at some point – skiing, snowboarding, and blowing the Alphorn . . . living the Heidi life."

"Switzerland is awesome," Clif said sadly. "I am afraid I may have already lost her."

Cal revealed shock as he said, "What? What happened? You two were perfect together."

Clif replied, "Gaby informed me she was pregnant – that I was going to be a father."

"Whoa!" Cal said. "That is unexpected news. Normally I would say fantastic and congratulations.

I'm guessing a mature couple like the two of you is suddenly struggling with the logistics of your future."

Clif shook his head. "She made it clear that I should sell the Lujon and move to Geneva. Living with me here was not an option."

"I'm not so sure she isn't right," Cal said. "What kind of life will Gaby and your child have living on a boat in the Delta, with dad chasing some of the world's nastiest bad guys. In Switzerland, your child will grow up speaking five languages, immersed in sports and the fine arts. I wish you two would adopt me."

Clif replied, "It is not a matter of whether she is right. She probably is right, but ultimatums bother me. I give in to her ultimatum and sooner than later, she'll hit me with another 'her-way-or-the-highway.' It's as though the child empowers her to be the decision maker 100% of the time, and her decisions are always correct and preeminent. I want a partner not a boss. Been there and done that with Susan."

"What about your obligation to be a full-time dad to your child?" Cal asked.

Clif said, "I'm aware of my responsibilities, but this pregnancy falls under the category of 'un-planned.' Gaby assured me she was on the pill and not ready to have children and settle down with me. We never discussed it. I am taking her word the baby is mine and not some hot-shot pilot for Swiss Air."

"Ouch," Cal said. "The very fact you are thinking along those lines is a bad sign. I wish I had some pithy, sage advice for you my friend, but I do not."

Brakemeyer sighed and said, "When I resolve the Sloughhouse Letters case and ex-wife lawsuit, I'll fly to Geneva and talk with Gaby."

Cal shook his head. "The baby could be celebrating a birthday before those two predicaments are resolved. You shouldn't wait. Make decisions now."

I'll never be a 'dead-beat' dad. You don't have to worry about that."

"In that case I do have some sage advice. Send her 'thinking of you' flowers. If you still care about her, you should let her know."

"Good advice," Brakemeyer said. "I'll arrange for flowers tomorrow first thing."

A dower Brakemeyer and sullen Calvin Chu both yawned at the same time. They smiled at each other acknowledging the curious nature of yawning contagion.

***

A deep-dive into the cerebration of Brakemeyer's circumstances brought the inevitable comparison of good and evil. The good took the form of excellent health and physical strength, a successful private security business, a very large bank account, a luxurious live-aboard yacht, and a lovely Swiss girlfriend.

An hour ago, he received a secret phone call from an anonymous source within the San Francisco City Police Department. The caller whispered news of a letter accusing Sam Lion of the murder of Roberto Spawn – the evil.

The accusation of murder sparked only minimal concern from the delta resident. After all, he was the only witness to the man drowning in San Francisco Bay, the supposed murder happened over two years ago, and no body of the supposed murder victim was ever found. Clif's eyewitness testimony declared self-defense, a factor suddenly overlooked by his former Chief. What bothered the retired detective most involved the name Sam Lion. Two years ago, his short-lived fame as an up-and-coming Bay Area artist found recognition through his *nom de plume* Sam Lion.

His cellphone sang 'Some Beach' by Blake Shelton signaling an incoming phone call. The screen announced his best friend, Calvin Chu.

"Hey Cal, what new crime am I accused of today? You want to come over and play chess?"

"I am coming over, but not to play chess," Cal replied. "Detective Karl is here on a mission from our favorite San Francisco Chief of Police. He wants to arrest both you and me."

"Oh, for god's sake," Brakemeyer declared.

He pondered Cal's ominous statement a moment. A sarcastic reply danced on the tip of his tongue. However, he found himself saying, "Bring him over here so we may discover *what has the Chief's panties in a wad*. I'll put on a fresh pot of coffee."

Calvin Chu lived on a 51-foot Blue Water Motoryacht berthed at Oxbow Marina on Georgiana Slough; his drive to Willow Berm would take only five or six minutes. Detective Karl, in his shit-colored, unmarked police car, followed Cal in his new black Ford Exhibition with all the bells and whistles available – a huge vehicle containing all the computer tech of a space ship.

Brakemeyer's one day off work per week usually took the form of fishing the delta's waters where salmon, catfish, and sturgeon were all possibilities in the winter. His freezer brimmed with fish sealed in *FoodSaver plastic* for future gourmand feasts. Occasionally, he played chess with Cal. Today, however, he gave a pass to even those wonderfully lazy forms of activity.

Brakemeyer took a longer sip of his hot chocolate as he worked his way around the side of the enclosed flybridge, and down into the bowels of the yacht where the galley's coffee maker stood ready to grind fresh beans and brew ten cups of delicious Columbian coffee.

Brakemeyer forced his video-playback thinker to ponder *acceptance.* His acceptance took the form of acknowledgment of his failures in life. He failed at marriage by wedding a manipulating dictator rather than a partner. After only six months of unrecognized bliss, his wife-boss fired him when his failure as a police detective made national news.

Police Detective Brakemeyer failed when he chose to save the life of a middle-aged, defenseless woman by eliminating an eighteen-year-old, knife-wielding crack head. He failed to consider the social and racial implications before shooting the young man threatening the life of a defenseless woman.

He failed again when his ex-wife attempted reconciliation. He ended her 'Cliffy' manipulations for the last time by tossing her into the murky waters of the Sausalito Yacht Harbor. The resulting lawsuit would likely shallow his pockets of cash. The retired Police Detective realized a better handling of his failures would have left him less troubled and a bit richer.

Brakemeyer knew that *revenge* sometimes exchanged places with the need for justice. Criminals he'd arrested, and a few that got away, likely held revenge for him in their twisted-with-evil minds. Bringing them to justice always meant acting within the bounds of legal jurisprudence.

During his days as a Navy Seal, missions against the enemy always protected his anonymity. He conducted war on his country's terms and conditions.

As a former police detective, he often stood front and center where evil looked him directly in the eyes. He knew only the scofflaws and seriously bad actors wanted revenge. Again, he conducted his job of peace officer and hunter of criminals according to his police department's terms and conditions. In this regard, his anonymity held no protection. An error of judgment or perceived error meant life-changing trouble with the public as well as the department.

As owner-operator of B-DELTA Security, a private security, risk management, and defense contracting company, justice enclosed broader terms and conditions imposed by dozens of cities, counties, states, and countries. This circumstance usually provided room to maneuver. For instance, to right the wrongs committed by the likes of the Nazi Herta Hildegund and her skinhead ilk, justice took the form of a sniper rifle with a single, long-range bullet. Justice protected the lives of others where revenge might not.

As he loaded the coffee maker with fresh water and beans, *responsibilities* meant more than managing an international security company. Just yesterday, Brakemeyer received an ultimatum from his Swiss girlfriend. She announced her pregnancy made possible by the delta yacht bum. He should liquidate all holdings, including the Lujon, and move to Geneva. A wedding and happy home in the big city would soon follow according to his long-distance girlfriend.

Brakemeyer loved his Swiss Miss. Her stunning beauty matched only by her sharp mind, kept the delta man in perpetual amour. He found no fault with Gaby Uhlmann other than her dislike for his lifestyle. Responsibility meant becoming a dutiful husband and father. Nevertheless, did it have to be her way or the highway?

Death, either his or the evil people he brought to justice, represented an inevitable repercussion of his work. If criminals were sweet and genial, death's consideration would be minimal. For Brakemeyer, his chosen vocation placed him face-to-face with the vicious, villainous, and corrupt side of human society. So be it, he thought. Fighting city hall for his freedom, however, placed an even greater risk before him – greater than acceptance, responsibility, and revenge. Death by imprisonment remained this gendarme's biggest worry.

***

San Francisco City Police Detective, Arkamun Karl, paced nervously around the enclosed flybridge deck of the Lujon. Clif and Cal sat quietly as their former partner exposed his nervousness in carrying out his Chief's orders.

"This is a serious situation," Detective Karl barked at Cal for the third time. "You failed to act upon the information given you by Clif. Now we have some mystery person signing a letter *Sun Tzu* and demanding justice for the man killed."

Cal said, “Stop pacing Karl. Sit down and have a soda or a cup of coffee. Cliff just made a fresh pot in the galley.”

Through chattering teeth Karl said, “It is freezing up here. Can’t we go inside where it’s warm?”

Clif said, “Follow me.” He led Karl and Cal down the interior steps to the main salon door. Once inside, he shoved a mug of hot coffee into everyone’s hand.

Cal raised his mug in a toast. “To crime busters,” he said.

Without joining in the toast, Detective Karl gratefully sipped the hot mud. He spoke while starring into the umber depths of the coffee.

“The Chief came down on me like a ton of bricks. It looks like the department deliberately tried to cover up the ‘manslaughter’ of Roberto Spawn to protect Clifton Brakemeyer. I knew nothing of Clif’s report.”

Cal spoke somewhat astonished. “There was no body, no witnesses besides Clif, and no proof of death. Spawn could have swum to shore and then run off to Arizona with a bar fly from the Tenderloin.

The assassin that tried to kill Brakemeyer might have been a drug-running yacht thief from El Salvador."

The subject of the Chief's ire interjected. Brakemeyer said, "This letter is a load of dreaming bullshit created by someone trying to send me to jail. The Chief is not interested in justice. He's simply frightened to death of bad public relations - again."

"None of us are in a position to second guess the Chief," Karl said.

"May we read this letter that accuses me of killing someone I don't know? Or should I call my lawyer right now?" Brakemeyer asked.

Karl squirmed, rolled his eyes, and handed the letter to Clif. He said, "It's anonymous but the details match exactly the report Detective Chu put in the computer when you called in the incident."

Brakemeyer examined the letter and the envelope stapled to it. Little details mattered.

"The envelope is postmarked 'Sloughhouse,'" he said. "That is very odd that the letter was mailed from a little community on the Cosumnes River just south of Sacramento."

Detective Karl yelled, "So what, Clif? The letter's contents are what the Chief is up in arms about."

Brakemeyer read the letter aloud:

"To the San Francisco City Police Department:

This letter is to notify you that Clifton Brakemeyer, a.k.a. Sam Lion, the Detective relieved of duty for killing an innocent young African American, also killed another innocent man on July 26 of the year before last. The deceased's name is Roberto Spawn of South San Francisco.

Roberto visited Brakemeyer living aboard Julia Delmar's yacht the Lujon at the Sausalito yacht Harbor to discuss a business agenda. Sam Lion-Clifton Brakemeyer piloted the boat to a point in the middle of the Bay of San Francisco; killed Mr. Spawn, and threw his body into the water. He then returned the ship to its dock in Sausalito. Brakemeyer cruelly followed the assassination of Mr. Spawn by dining with Beverly Wells at the Jardinière restaurant in San Francisco. We seek justice for the victims.

"Victory is reserved for those who are willing to pay its price.

Sun Tzu"

Brakemeyer said, "You are a better detective than you are letting on Karl. The vague information in this letter *does not* match the story I told detective Chu on the night of July 26. I told Cal that someone put a bag over my head and sapped me from behind. I awoke to find myself bound hand and foot with a ten-pound barbell weight duct taped to my feet.

The yet unseen assassin piloted Julia's yacht to the middle of the Bay. After the killer dragged me down the steps to the aft swim platform, I kick him in the face. He fell into the bay and sank. I crawled back up the steps and broke the glass gate panel. A shard of glass enabled me to cut my bonds.

I turned on the Lujon's running lights and used a spot to search for the man I kicked into the bay. Not finding him, I called Cal, related the details of what happened, and then returned the Lujon to its berth in the yacht harbor. A concussion and pitch-black night prevented me from identifying the man trying to kill me. All I can say is he was big and very strong."

Calvin Chu said, "Brakemeyer could not identify or even describe his assailant. The man that attacked him could have been anybody."

"Why in god's name didn't you file a report the way you should have?" Karl asked Detective Chu.

Cal said, "Precisely because of what is happening now. The Chief would have freaked out and prevented Clif from pursuing Ramey and Poe."

"When I met Beverly Wells at the restaurant," Brakemeyer said, "Niles Ramey showed up. The person that sent this letter must have worked with him and Frederick Mahler. Ramey called me 'killer' and no doubt reported his encounter with me. Ramey knew that Spawn's orders involved killing me, which did not happen. This letter is describing what Spawn was supposed to do to me. Ramey had a partner named Willie Poe that never experienced prosecution for the Mahler affair due to lack of evidence. He and Frederick Mahler's shadow, Acucena Cascalho, disappeared after the big dust up at the Hunter's Point warehouse."

Karl said, “We discovered that the Cascalho woman returned to her native Brazil. She is a wealthy heiress or something.”

Brakemeyer descended into his memory of the Brazilian bombshell. Her long black hair fell in natural waves to her shoulders and down her back. Her creamy, light brown skin complimented long, curved eyebrows, large and slightly sleepy-looking dark brown eyes, and long-long, black eyelashes. Cascalho’s lips were not overly puffy but a perfect heart shape, wide and lovely.

She smiled rarely but when she did, her bright teeth spoke of love and passion, joy and mischievousness. The woman’s figure looked sturdy and athletic. Brakemeyer remembered her stunning and sexy beauty totally offset by her relentless chatter about the world ending due to overpopulation. Her oratory shrank Brakemeyer’s compulsion to fawn over the Brazilian bachelorette. He chose instead to avoid the pedantic gallery owner at all costs. She demonstrated a cold and almost ‘zombie-like’ ill will for human life.

Brakemeyer read the letter again in silence. He asked, “What is the bio on Roberto Spawn?”

Detective Karl grudgingly pulled another sheet from his portfolio case and handed it to the former detective. Both Brakemeyer and Chu knew Karl played a good cop, bad cop game while giving them all the information he possessed about the situation.

Brakemeyer scanned the document. He said, “This reads like William Bonney’s rap sheet. Spawn did time for assault, manslaughter, attempted murder, and extortion. He showed no signs of support and yet lived quite well in a view apartment in South San Fran. Cash must have covered his life style since he possessed no bank accounts, investments, or retirement.”

“He definitely fell under the category of ‘bad actor,’” Karl said. “We have learned that he has been missing since the third week in July a year ago.”

“It is safe to say he is the assassin I kicked into the bay,” Brakemeyer admitted. “My guess is he, Ramey, and Poe worked as a team. The three of them pulled off the robbery and murder of Johnny McCall at the Wicks estate in the Delta. You will likely find Mr. Spawn a member of the gay gym ‘Muscelheads’ on Polk Street.”

"I will check that out," Karl said. "In the meantime, I'm ordered to place the both of you under arrest. You're not going to fight me on this are you?"

"You're arresting us – at this time of day?" Cal asked in astonishment.

"That's my job fellas. Clif killed a man and you failed to file a report which means a reprimand at the very least."

"Let's get this straight," Brakemeyer said. "As a former Navy SEAL and San Francisco City Police Detective, I am no longer a credible witness to an attempt on my life. With my hands tied behind my back, my ankles taped to a ten-pound weight, and gag over my mouth I kicked a man about to throw me in the Bay. He fell in the water instead of me and did not surface as far as I know. I reported the assassination attempt; and I'm being arrested and charged with manslaughter or murder based on an anonymous letter full of lies, and misstatement of facts?"

Karl stammered and said, "I didn't say you are being charged with manslaughter or whatever. Come on Clif, you know the law must be satisfied. It must declare your actions 'justifiable' so the case can be closed."

"Until someone decides that justifiable should be manslaughter," Brakemeyer said with bitterness. "I've been this route before."

"I'm just doing my job fellas," Karl complained.

"When the Chief came down on you like a ton of bricks," Brakemeyer asked, "what was his position on charges? Did he want me processed for possible justifiable homicide; or did he want me charged with manslaughter and held for a hearing? It matters to my attorney."

"Manslaughter," Karl answered sadly. "The Chief was very angry, mostly over finding out about what happened now instead of a couple years ago."

"Karl," Brakemeyer said earnestly, "please allow Cal and I the dignity of turning ourselves in tomorrow so we may avoid detention and bring our attorneys along. I mean, does the Chief really want us behind bars that badly?"

Arkamun Karl pinched his lips and set down his coffee mug. "You are asking a lot Clif. The Chief will ream my ass for not following his explicit orders. I'll never see another promotion in his lifetime."

Both Brakemeyer and Chu remained silent but bore their penetrating gazes down upon Detective Karl. They waited until Karl finally broke.

"Okay! Okay!" He yelled. "I give up! If you're not in the Chief's office at 9:00 a.m. sharp, I'll ream *your* ass, and drag you both to the station in handcuffs!"

Karl knew that last boast held zero chance in reality and made him look as foolish as he felt. The two arrestees smiled.

Clif said, "Thank you Detective. You're a better man than your boss. We'll be on time with bells on."

After Karl exited the yacht, he left the Willow Berm Marina for the return drive to San Francisco. Cal stepped to the galley and refilled his coffee mug.

"Guess you'll have to give me a ride back to my humble cruiser at Oxbow in that crazy hot Corvette of yours."

"My pleasure as always," Brakemeyer replied. "I'll pick you up at seven tomorrow morning for the traffic battle into San Fran. We can't let Detective Karl down, or the Chief of Police for that matter."

"The Chief can bite me," Cal replied.

At sunset, no one at the marina paid any attention to the man that jogged three miles on Brannan Island Road to the B & W Resort Marina, crossed Georgiana Slough with a powerful crawl stroke, and then ran Tyler Island Road to Oxbow Marina. The man once again swam across and around the big bow in Georgiana Slough until he entered the covered berths of the marina. He pulled himself out of the water on the swim step of the Delta Junk.

Clif often substituted his daily workout for the run-swim-run conditioning required to reach Cal's boat at Oxbow Marina. He decided to question his best friend as casually as possible, as though he did not care one way or the other. The man could get touchy on certain subjects.

Cal appeared on the aft flybridge deck and peered down at his friend on the swim step. "You dropped me off in your Corvette, drove back to your boat, and then returned here by swimming the river? What the hell?"

"I ran most of the way," Clif replied. "Karl was right; it is freezing out here. How about a towel and some hot chocolate?"

Cal scowled and said, "It's almost dark! Now I must drive you back to your boat. You are really annoying sometimes, you know?"

Brakemeyer toweled off the river water, donned the terry cloth robe from Cal's swim locker, and headed for the Delta Junk's galley. After settling into the dining booth, he launched into his query.

"You and Doctor May Tockterman resembled a one-way trip to the alter. What happened? You haven't spoken about her in weeks."

"After you created B-DELTA Security," Cal responded sadly, "May and I began to differ on my role in your new business. I had not finished my six months of testing for the AIDS virus yet. She seemed to think that I might have the deadly disease; I should remain sheltered creating no risk to myself or others. Discussion turned to argument, which turned to a kind of estrangement. She said she couldn't live with me on a boat in the delta. She had to *work on herself.*"

"She did not hand you that corny line, did she? You're telling me that May was less afraid of a deadly virus than she was of your joining me in my private security company?"

"All my tests have been negative – by some miracle," Cal said.

Brakemeyer shook his head in astonishment. "We employ fourteen, combat-ready private soldiers of which you and I are the managers. May was afraid of that?"

Cal dodged the question by saying, "We really miss Marcs." "She knew how to conduct operations as well as anyone. Have you experienced any success in finding her replacement?"

Brakemeyer shook his head. "I am sorry you and May split. You two were good together. As for a replacement for Commander Marcs, no luck so far. I've promoted Johnson to temporary commander to keep the unit trained and ready.

"Cal," Brakemeyer said, "the letter to the department is very peculiar. Someone is messing with you and me in a very dangerous way. Everyone connected with the Frederick Mahler affair is in trouble.

Beverly Wells possesses Mahler's documents as well as the Julia Delmar exposé letter. The lists of players in the Defenders of Jasoom are all in trouble, not to mention you, me, and Beverly."

***

The showing for modern artist Joáo Matheus resembled a large soiree for a movie star. His paintings and sculptures filled the lower floor of the Ipanema Galeria owned and operated by Acucena Cascalho. Tables of food filled every corner, a glass of champagne decorated each empty hand, and Brazilian pop rock blared from ceiling speakers in every room.

An 80-year-old building on Rua Anibal Mendonça less than a block from Ipanema Beach held the Galeria as a museum holds a traveling exhibit. Its eye-catching yellow exterior drew crowds akin to a bowl of ripe pineapple chunks drawing ravens and sparrows. The interior boasted eggshell-colored walls with spotlights on each work of art. With strategically placed Victorian furniture, the Galeria felt more like an English manor than an art showplace.

Acucena Cascalho, called Cena by most people, knew how to sell artwork. She created demand by embroiling the artist in some form of controversy that made the papers and social media glow. She created events surrounding the artist that made purchasing his or her work a cultural necessity. Artwork from her gallery filled the homes of the rich and famous, hospitals, attorney's offices, and the suites of corporate executives throughout Rio and Sao Paulo.

Cena did not wait for customers to come to her but constantly reached out through the internet, social media, and newspapers. Her showings were often as much about the customers as the artist and his or her work.

No one knew she played a key role in the theft of artwork from around the world, selling forgeries, defrauding museums and galleries, and murdering art-world professionals that might reveal her secrets and those of her eidolon, the late Frederick Mahler. She acted as Mahler's proctor or seneschal for a group of art thieves calling themselves the Defenders of

Jasoom. Her purpose was Mahler's purpose - to kill half the world's population through disease infestation.

Clifton Brakemeyer destroyed that goal which eventually led to the death of Frederick Mahler. For Acucena Cascalho, Clifton Brakemeyer, known in the San Francisco art community as Sam Lion, needed Execução or execution along with Beverly Wells, Ranjeet Bhabananda, the other members of the Defenders of Jasoom, and Julia Delmar's company Global International, Inc. Cena would see to their punishment in her own special way. Despite laws to the contrary, she wholeheartedly believed that her morality was not only correct but also justified. She would punish her enemies.

Cena quietly slipped away from the party and her host duties. From the sanctity of her office on the second floor, she pulled a seldom-used cell phone from her antique oak desk's center drawer. Cena tapped in a phone number and waited.

"I'm here, what's up boss?" Willie Poe said.

"Did Global International receive my letter?" she asked.

"Yeah, boss, CEO Blevins received it. Yesterday, I gave him a special surprise when his cargo container ship cleared the Golden Gate Bridge and entered the Bay."

"Tomorrow I'll email to you the text for your next letter. We don't need any more letters to Blevins or his company Global International. I am almost finished with them. Make certain you are ready for a visit from Sam Lion or his team of private soldiers."

"Yes mam," Willie answered dutifully.

***

Brakemeyer stood alongside his attorney, Oscar Fluteman, and waited. Calvin Chu stood next to his attorney Archie Fanchon Arrowsmith. Archie, classified by Cal as a *knockout* lady of the law, recently switched her legal practice from intellectual property specialist to criminal law. She ripped Chief Brown a new one. He dismissed Cal but placed a reprimand on his record with the department for failing to file a report on the Brakemeyer incident. Archie could not talk the angry Chief out of that action.

Cal winked at Brakemeyer and proudly strolled from the Chief's office with his attorney. Clif whispered to him as he passed.

"I understand your attorney's husband is a tough advertising executive not to be trifled with."

"You really know how to buzz kill a man's fantasy don't you? See you back at the boat."

When the award-winning counselor for B-Delta Security finished his exculpation of Brakemeyer's actions against an unknown assailant, the San Francisco City Police Chief acted more irritated than relieved.

"My only concern, Counselor," he said, "is the social media threat posed in the letter. What am I to do if Sam Lion is exposed as ex-detective Clifton Brakemeyer, and is involved in another killing that took place over two years ago?"

Oscar replied, "Put Roberto Spawn's record on display; put your PR people to work claiming you've been looking for Spawn for over two years to arrest him on suspicion of murder of Mr. Johnathon McCall. The link between Brakemeyer and Spawn is not provable. You are convinced ex-Navy SEAL and

San Francisco City Police Detective Clifton Brakemeyer almost died at the hands of drug mules trying to steal the yacht he was leasing from Julia Delmar. You get the idea."

Brakemeyer broke in and said, "Chief, my art career as Sam Lion never took off. Being exposed should not be too large a burden. I can move my boat around so the media can't locate me easily."

Oscar Fluteman lifted his briefcase and said to the Chief, "Mr. Brakemeyer is free to go? You are closing the incident as 'justifiable homicide?'"

The Chief replied, "No Counselor – Mr. Brakemeyer remains a 'person of interest' in an open case. The Roberto Spawn missing person case remains open until he or his body turns up. If Spawn is found to have died as a result of foul play, then all bets are off."

"You really don't like my client, do you Chief Brown?"

"Like or don't like does not apply. I follow the law."

"As long as it meets your political agenda," Fluteman said. "Mr. Brakemeyer is innocent of illegalities Chief Brown. His business brings him into contact with dangerous characters. What more do you demand of a properly licensed detective that carries a firearm, and defends himself when threatened with bodily harm? You should consider him an adjunct to the police department, not an enemy."

The Chief sat stone faced unwilling to comment. Brakemeyer followed his attorney out of the building.

As the two men stood on the sidewalk watching cars pass, Oscar Fluteman said, "I don't think Chief Brown is done with you. He insisted you vanish into obscurity after the shooting of the crack head. Instead, Sam Lion a.k.a. Clifton Brakemeyer lived like a millionaire and continued to stir the pot in far too public a manner."

"Those millions arrived in my bank account as a result of several near-death experiences. A cab crash caused by an assassin's bullet, a beating with several cracks to my head, and gunfire that nearly tore a hole in my torso should be worth something."

"As a San Francisco Police officer and detective, you used to deal with near death experiences for sixty grand a year."

Brakemeyer smiled and said, "Actually, I benefited from the largess of a powerful woman executive with a guilty conscience. Luck covered me like coastal fog."

Oscar said, "You are also lucky that I am a very good attorney."

"If you're so good," Brakemeyer said sarcastically, "Why haven't you shaken my ex-wife off my tail? I could use one less problem to worry about."

"The proceedings with your ex should come to a conclusion fairly soon," Oscar said. "I have filed a counter suit against her for harassment in the amount of attorney's fees plus $10,000. This will force a court hearing in front of a judge. Judges understand gold digging when they see it. She'll settle."

"She is the queen of gold diggers, and a great actress too. She'll play up my tossing her in the yacht basin water, the trauma, the heartache, the mental pain and anguish. Susan will make it sound like the sinking of the Titanic when she's done."

Oscar smiled and said, “She will truly have mental pain and anguish when I’m done with her. Rest easy my boy. She’ll settle.”

Four
A New Member of the Team

The two owners of B-DELTA Security sat in the galley booth of Cal's Bluewater Coastal Cruiser the Delta Junk. They sipped late afternoon highballs consisting of Jack Daniels and Seven Up. They re-hashed their day's business.

Brakemeyer's cell phone sounded. He answered and said, "Yes, Mr. Blevins – what's up?"

He listened for several minutes as Blevins gave him a complete briefing of the destruction of Global International's shipping containers.

"Cal and I will assemble a team. Tomorrow morning, we shall scan the sight thoroughly for clues. Is the Oakland Police Department on sight?"

He listened and then said, "It might be a good idea if you meet us there to help breach any bureaucratic road blocks. Did my two security men check in with you before going covert? Good, thank you sir."

Cal asked, "The boss has a job for us?"

"Yes," Brakemeyer said. "Yesterday, someone blew up all four of Global International's cargo containers on the container ship Achelois as it entered San Francisco Bay. The destroyed connex's have been set aside at the Port of Oakland along with the surrounding damaged containers. Blevins received a letter a few days ago threating his life. It was signed 'Sun Tzu' - same paper, same computer, same postmark as the Chief's letter."

Cal said, "Whoa – that certainly removes any credibility for the letter sent to the police department."

"Credibility – yes, but that letter produced the sender's desired effect. It put me under a microscope; one wrong move and I'm toast."

Brakemeyer explained, "Blevins's letter means two things - one, there is purposeful intent behind these letters of destruction, and two, I better perform my best sales job on Nick Falkenrath. We really need the help of his BND significant other."

Brakemeyer departed Cal's company and returned to the Lujon. The head of B-DELTA Security worked from his office in the former crew cabin on the starboard side of level one. As Brakemeyer walked, he pulled his cell phone and used his voice to call his recent client Nicholas Falkenrath.

"Falkenrath home and office fittings," Nick answered even though he could see Brakemeyer's name on his cell phone screen.

"Mr. Falkenrath, this is Clifton Brakemeyer calling to ask you a big favor."

"I don't owe you money, do I?" Nick asked.

"No, no nothing like that," Brakemeyer said. "I have a very difficult case staring me in the face. Having lost Commander Marcs, I could really use the expertise of Colonel Schmidt. Would the two of you agree to help me out?"

Nick replied, "I thank you for the courtesy of asking me first Mr. Brakemeyer. Would your case be especially dangerous? I'd hate to agree to Ada dashing in harm's way."

"As you know, anything is possible. I need her experience with explosives. My primary client lost four container loads of products from India and the far east."

Nick said, "Whoa that sounds serious. To tell you the truth, Ada's been bored stupid since moving in with me. She works out every day and rides my 650cc Suzuki dirt bike in the mountains. I've been so busy at my factory I haven't peeled out any time for her besides dinner and a movie. I'll give you her direct cell number."

"Thank you, Nick. I shall call her right now. The work is in the Port of Oakland. She'll be staying next to Jack London Square on my boat if she agrees. Thanks again."

"Just one question," Nick said. "Are you married or have a significant other on your boat? When it comes to Ada, falling in love with her is pretty easy; you are even a bigger stud than me."

Brakemeyer laughed and said, "I am in the middle of being sued by my ex-wife. My significant other is a beautiful and charming Swiss lady named Gabriel Uhlmann. Currently, she is flying somewhere in the world with Swiss Air, but is definitely my long-term soul mate. You have no worries on my account. Oh, and thank you for the complement."

Brakemeyer phoned Ada's private number. She answered immediately.

"Colonel Schmidt, this is Clifton Brakemeyer. Nick suggested I call you directly with my offer of temporary employment. You would have to be an independent contractor – take care of your own taxes."

"Nick is trying to get rid of me already," Ada said laughing.

Brakemeyer chuckled and said, "He's very concerned that you are bored stupid and could use a little excitement for a few days."

"Does this have anything to do with the loss of Commander Marcs?"

Brakemeyer answered, "Yes it does, Colonel. I miss her expertise and until I can find a replacement, I could use your help."

Ada did not hesitate. She said, "Okay, I am 'in' Mr. Brakemeyer – when and where?"

"I suggest driving from your home near Jobs Peak to the Waterfront Hotel in Jack London Square.

You'll be living aboard my boat for a few days. It will be docked on the long pier behind the hotel."

Ada said, "I'll talk with Nick, pack my bags, and be on my way. I'll see you in five hours."

The retired German agent packed three days' worth of work clothing, footwear, a few cleverly disguised self-defense weapons, her passport, visa, and bath kit. She piled her luggage and herself into her new Ford Mustang Bullitt, the 5.0-liter, 480 horsepower V8 muscle car. She test drove the Shelby GT350R with more horsepower but settled on the Bullitt for looks, interior esthetics, and a smooth shifting, 6-speed stick. The car's designers aimed their efforts creating a namesake for Steve McQueen's Mustang Fastback in the 1968 movie 'Bullitt.' The best description of their results with this Mustang was 'bad-ass.'

Her dark Highland Green Bullitt looked uncompromising and dangerous and cruised easily at 130 miles per hour. Ada learned this as she and Nick enjoyed a maiden voyage on Highway 50, Nevada's loneliest highway. During one hair-raising stretch of empty road, she set the Bullitt's engine to screaming upon reaching its maximum of 165 miles per hour. Ada delighted in the speed, handling, and white cue ball gearshift knob.

Falkenrath Home and Office Fittings became Ada's only stop on her drive to Oakland. She chatted a bit with Nick and absorbed all his concerns about working with an international security company pursuing a mad bomber. Falkenrath's anxiety attached itself to the knowledge his fiancé loved her work as an undercover agent for the German BND.

The adventure of busting bad guys and risking her life held no equal. Without dangerous excitement Ada's existence remained quietly unfulfilled. As the former BND Agent prepared to depart, Nick gave Ada the most passionate hug and kiss he could muster. The memory of it remained with her all the way to Oakland.

The Bullitt's navigation computer screen spoke to Ada occasionally giving her updates on the route to her destination in Jack London Square. She crossed Donner Summit and descended Interstate 80 to the Sacramento Valley minding the speed limits.

Colonel Schmidt quickly realized that traveling the speed limit placed her with the slower moving trucks, campers, and overly cautious drivers clogging the right lane. She decided to match the speed of traffic in the passing lane allowing her to shift from third to fourth gear and engage her fellow travelers in a little friendly competition on the Interstate speedway.

Upon reaching Oakland, as if by magic, Clifton Brakemeyer appeared at the Washington Street entrance to Jack London's Waterfront Parking Garage. He waived down Ada before she could turn into the garage to get lost in six-stories of auto labyrinth.

Brakemeyer opened the passenger door and climbed in. He said, "Hi, Colonel. Nice to see you again. Nice wheels."

"Thanks," Ada replied. "Nice to see you again, I think."

"I've moved the Lujon to a nearby bulkhead running laterally from the end of the marina pier just aft of the gas dock," Clif stated. "Go around the block and I'll direct you to free parking on the opposite side of the train tracks. Then we'll get you settled in the stateroom amidships – unless you'd prefer another location on the yacht."

"The amidships stateroom will be fine," Ada said.

Brakemeyer said, "My partner, Calvin Chu, will be staying in the crew's quarters behind your room and across the hall from my office."

"And where do you rest your head commander?"

"I'm one floor up in the forward master stateroom." Clif directed Ada to a parking location. "Ah, turn left here and drive straight for two blocks. I am pleased you don't mind the stateroom far from mine. I prefer you be a reasonable distance away from me for tactical reasons."

Ada lifted an eyebrow and said, "I sincerely hope we both share the same definition of tactical."

The owner of B-DELTA Security laughed. "I assured Nick that my current romantic entanglement precludes any accidental, non-business intoxication with you. That's why I shall address you as Colonel Schmidt at all times."

The pair of sleuths parked the Bullitt two spaces from Clif's ZR1 Corvette and hiked the fifty yards to the marina dock. After a short distance, Ada decided to ask the personal question.

"Do you care to illuminate on your romantic entanglement as you put it?"

Clif replied, "Did you notice my new Vette? You like fast cars I see. My new ZR1 has a 6.2-liter V8 generating 755 horsepower at 6300 r.p.m.'s. Top speed is 210 m.p.h."

"Clever dodge of my question," Ada said.

Clif hesitated and then said, "I will only say her name is Gabrielle Uhlmann from Geneva, Switzerland. Some night in the future you and Nick can get me drunk and I'll spill the whole sordid story and my life-altering quandary."

Ada said, "Maybe I should get you drunk before discussing my contractual payment for this job."

Brakemeyer smiled and said, "My partner, Calvin Chu, has your paperwork ready at the boat. You will receive our standard pay scale plus a bonus and hazard pay should that unlikely event take place. The CEO of Global International is not a piker when it comes to my services. You will meet him tomorrow. I'll bet we pay better than the BND."

Ada chuckled and said, "I must brush up on my American colloquialisms – 'piker?'"

***

The dispossessed vagrant slowly stepped down Clay Street in Oakland carrying his wrinkled paper bag exposing the neck of a cheap bottle of wine. His shredded pants hung on him like a rodeo clown's barrel and suspenders. Shaggy brown hair poked out from under a rumpled men's sun hat. The man's stained, brown beard matched his hair. Round dark sunglasses sat on a bulbous nose. A dirty, tan trench coat hid the vagrant's overall large size.

He ambled down the building's side next to the railroad tracks, and then behind the Global International store. Sitting with his back against the wall next to a small tree, he pretended to swig the wine while watching for passers-by.

After ten minutes the homeless man stood, pushed the empty wine bottle into the bag so as not to draw the attention of another hopeful itinerant, wedged the bag at the bottom of the roll up cargo door, and slowly stepped away without looking back.

He already performed this same routine at the Global store in Serramonte Center in Daly City, Bridgepointe Parkway in San Mateo, and Mount Diablo Boulevard in Walnut Creek.

The vagrant shuffled two blocks to a rusty van parked in the loading zone of another store. He noticed two young street thugs looking in the windows of the van.

"Beat it punks," he yelled.

"Yo bro, what's the problemo?" one of the toughs said. "We beat yo ass fucka."

The vagrant ran up to the two street sharks and attacked them savagely. He punched and kicked for every vital body part they possessed.

One kid hit the pavement clutching his damaged throat. The other tough screamed as the vagrant kicked his left kneecap loose. Just as quickly, the homeless-looking man climbed behind the driver's wheel of the van, started the engine, and then roared off down the boulevard. He laughed as he stripped off his wig and fake nose, and drove northeast toward Sacramento.

***

The thunderclap that brought Brakemeyer and Ada Schmidt out of their berths and running for the main lounge had nothing to do with stormy weather. The night sky shone with city-light dimmed stars and a moon the size of a dinner plate.

"That sounded like a lightning bolt and really close," Brakemeyer said.

"Sounded like ordinance to me," Ada remarked.

Brakemeyer said, "Oh god, there is a Global International store very close to us. It is on Clay Street a few blocks from here. I think we had better check it out. Do you mind, Colonel?"

"Give me a few minutes to dress," Ada replied.

Both Brakemeyer and Ada dressed and met in berth disguised as a small office. The private detective sat at a small desk with an iBUYPOWER Trace 9220 gaming computer and then brought up a police and fire department app. Calling Police Scanner 5-0, he tapped a series of keys and the program brought up 'Police,' 'Fire,' and 'EMS.' Brakemeyer turned up the audio volume on the computer and then selected 'Police.'

The program scanned the radio airwaves until it landed on the Oakland Police frequency. The two detectives listened intently.

Squawk . . . "Baker 9 – be advised that there are three other terrorist explosions. All attacks happened at Global International stores in San Mateo, Daly City, and Walnut Creek."

Squawk . . . "10-4 control. We have the Clay Street store."

Squawk . . . Baker 9 - Fire and ambulances are in route."

Squawk . . . "10-4 control. We need PG&E here. The substation across the street from the store is in danger. There may be power lines down. We need back up to set up road blocks on Clay, Embarcadero West, and 2nd Street."

Clif and Ada listened for several more minutes before deciding to check out the damage for themselves. They jogged to Clif's Corvette in the parking lot and drove toward the fire glow and smoke mushroom.

When they were still two blocks away, Alameda and Oakland Police cars blocked the street. Their flashing red, white, and blue lights streaked the surrounding buildings. The sirens of fire trucks screamed from several blocks away. The Global International store roared with flames threatening surrounding structures and the power utility sub-station.

After parking Clif's Corvette, the pair of sleuths strode with purpose toward the action. An Oakland City Police Officer stopped them.

"Hold it right there," the female officer said. "Why are you folks here at this time of night?"

"My name is Clifton Brakemeyer and this is Colonel Ada Schmidt. We are with Global International's Security Company B-DELTA Security International. Global International is my client. Here is my I.D. and business card. Colonel Schmidt is on loan from Germany's BND."

The officer examined Ada's passport and said, "What's a BND? Never heard of it."

Ada said, “It is Germany’s equivalent of America’s FBI. I am retired from their International Division.”

“The officer shined her flashlight in Ada’s face. “You look pretty young to be retired. All right,” the officer said. “Proceed to the building but don’t get too close and don’t get in the way.”

Clif and Ada hiked up 2nd Street to a point across from the rear of Global’s retail store. They watched the fire team dump huge streams of water on the burning section. They created a water wall barrier between the fire and the electrical substation. Sparks flew from broken power lines only 30 yards away.

“That took a big chunk of Semtex to blow a hole in the ground as well as a third of the building,” Brakemeyer said.

Ada said, “I would say the bomber used C-4 since it is a lot easier to buy or steal. Some type of accelerant like auto petrol would account for the fire. It would appear that all four bombs detonated at exactly the same time meaning synchronized actuators. Someone really hates Global International.”

Clif said, "We have a few hours before meeting the team at the Ports of America outer harbor. They began a forensic examination of the bombed containers yesterday and should finish today. Let's go back to the Lujon. I have letters from the bomber that you need to examine."

At 4:30 a.m., the two sleuths settled in the Lujon's main salon with cups of coffee and earnest attitudes. The Lujon's newest guest did not react to the luxury of the yacht around her but made mental notes of the location of furniture and stairwells. Ada carefully read the letters to the police department and to CEO Blevins of Global International. She examined images of the letters sent to Beverly Wells and the deceased Ranjeet Bhabananda.

"My English is not as good as my French," Ada said. "Something seems off about the content, or maybe it is the way the sentences are phrased."

Brakemeyer added, "I noticed that too. The envelope postmarks are from a small town south of Sacramento."

Ada examined the envelope and said, "Slough-house – an interesting name but an odd place to post letters."

"It's right next door to Rancho Murieta."

"What is a Rancho Murieta, another town?"

"I'm not certain whether it's incorporated or not. Rancho Murieta is a massive bedroom community development. It's all track houses, duplexes, small lakes, and golf courses."

"All roads lead to Rome and all these letters lead to you, Clifton Brakemeyer."

"The letter to Robert Blevins was not aimed at me," Brakemeyer said. "It clearly targeted President Blevins and his company."

"And who is the private detective detail for the Global International Company?" Ada asked.

"I see your point."

"Time to 'back and fill' Mr. Brakemeyer," Ada said smiling. "I believe you should inform me of your history with this Spawn character and Robert Blevins. The information may help me help you."

Brakemeyer rose from the tan leather sofa and retrieved the coffee pot from the galley. After pouring he and Ada a second cup of strong, black brew he sat down, sipped, and began his recap.

"I call this the Johnny McCall – J. Gordon Wicks case. About two years ago, I engaged an early morning contest with the fish in Snodgrass Slough in the Sacramento Delta. Instead of a fish, I snagged Johnny McCall. His killers tazed him, killed him, and then dumped him in the slough with weights tied around his feet. Though I no longer held a detective position with the San Francisco Police Department; I felt a strong need to help Johnny's killers find justice."

"Where does Gordon Wicks enter the picture," Ada asked.

"Johnny worked as a security guard for a very important Delta Rancher named J. Gordon Wicks. From my youth working ranches in the summer, I knew Wicks to be an arrogant ass. The ranch's previous owner, Julia Broderick Delmar founded and owned Global International Incorporated. She decided to help Wicks out of a financial jam by hiring me to find relics stolen from the Wick's ranch."

Ada asked, "By Johnny's killers?"

"Exactly," Clif replied. "It turned out that Julia Delmar involved herself with a group of art thieves funding a crazy scheme to spread contagion across the world."

"What?" Ada gasped.

"Oh, you have no idea what these monomaniacs were up to," Brakemeyer said. "A world-renown art dealer named Frederick Mahler built a laboratory and warehouse to breed and infect mosquitos and Tse-Tse flies with a dozen or so deadly diseases. He planned to load the insects into empty fifty-foot trailers in dozens of truck-trailer rigs, and then dump them out at various points around the U.S. The money made from stolen art and fraudulent art sales financed several other disease factories in countries with big populations like Mexico, India, China, and Africa."

"You prevented Frederick Mahler from executing his plan?" Ada asked.

Brakemeyer shook his head sadly. "My former detective partner, Calvin Chu and Julia Delmar, were captured by Niles T. Ramey and thrown naked into one of the trailers. I managed to save Cal but Julia

Delmar succumbed to the bites of hundreds of thousands of insects."

Ada said, "Please tell me Niles T. Ramey did not escape justice."

"He killed Johnny McCall and several other people connected to the art thefts. He narrowly missed killing me in Boston, and a journalist in Switzerland. He owned a real mean streak. He and I fought until I ripped his knee and broke his ankle. Eventually I shot him; I released the insects pumped into the truck when I saved Cal. The insects finished Ramey."

"I've been involved in some crazy cases over the years," Ada said, "but never anything as horrible as what you just described. Any other players in the game that might be out for revenge?"

"Potential victims beside me include one of the art thieves, Ranjeet Bhabananda. He shot and killed Frederick Mahler and received a short jail sentence for manslaughter. The Hindi art-gallery owner received the first letter laced with deadly toxins. Beverly Wells is a journalist with connections to Julia Delmar. Julia betrayed her fellow art thieves by sending an exposé letter to Beverly. My friend Calvin Chu was part of the team that brought down the population killers."

"Who is remaining from the list of bad guys?" Ada pushed for an answer.

"Ramey's partner, Roberto Spawn, took a swim in the Bay with help from my boot in his face. He is gone. Ramey's other partner, Willie Poe, escaped prosecution. He is big, nasty, and just about as sick in the head as Ramey was. He vanished into the ether but he is out there."

Brakemeyer put up his hand to stop the conversation. He rose and disappeared down a flight of stairs and into a side room berth he used to store files. The big security expert returned to his German guest, sat, and opened a file.

"Okay, okay, you want the remaining bad guys that might be targets for assassination or they may belong to the revenge bombers," Clif said.

"At least I didn't have to point my pistol at you to get an answer," Ada said with a smile.

Brakemeyer remembered Nick Falkenrath's comment about falling in love with Ada Schmidt. He understood why his former client felt as he did about the retired German secret agent. Her bearing carried a fearlessness born of many dangerous encounters. Thick blonde hair, sparkling blue eyes, dimples, and lovely thick lips with a dip in the center rounded off a face marred only by a small scar on the bottom of her chin. Her German accent reminded him of Gaby in a very endearing way.

Clif began reading from the file. "Members of the Defenders of Jasoom now dead include Frederick Mahler, Dr. Helmut Mueller, Derrick Pullman, Avery McMichaels, Julia Delmar, Louis D'Arceau, Niles T. Ramey, Aaron Broderick, and Roberto Spawn. Members in jail include J. Gordon Wicks and Ranjeet Bhabananda. Members that eluded justice include Sheldon A. Bathingswait, Marcel Karelle, Nashwa Zahur, William Poe, Mary Ellis Pike, and Acucena Cascalho. Cascalho functioned as Frederick Mahler's number two, and every bit the population reductionist fanatic. She could bury every warm body on the planet and not think twice about it."

"You know her?" Ada suggested.

"I met her once, on this yacht as a matter of fact," Clif replied. "She possessed a *musk* of sensuality that attracted listeners and an authoritarian command born of running businesses and managing money."

Ada mused a moment and then said, "The kind of woman that will always maintain loyal followers, especially men. We crossed paths with a certain woman named Herta Hildegund."

Brakemeyer said, "As you know, I have no response to that. Cascalho possesses much more intelligence and experience, and much less maniacal ego than the reposing Herta Hildegund."

"If she held the position of Mahler's number two, love as well as fanatical devotion to his vision might make her our number one suspect. Do we know her location?"

"Last report placed her in her villa in Joá, Rio de Janeiro, Brazil," Clif answered. "She owns a building with an art gallery next to Ipanema Beach. She is rich; that is all I know without deep-diving into her bio."

Ada asked, “What is your plan Detective? Do we start at the bottom and work up or start at the top and work down?”

“A bit of both,” Clif replied. “In a few hours we re-examine the blown containers at the Port of Oakland, and then travel to Sloughhouse to perform reconnaissance. After that, we work our way through the still-living members of the Defenders of Jasoom. We find ‘em, grill ‘em, and spill ‘em. The killer is in there somewhere.”

“And perhaps stock up on suntan lotion and beachwear,” Ada said. “I believe we will be heading to Rio sooner or later.”

SLOUGHHOUSE, CA
NOV 05 2020
USPS

Five
The Fifth Letter

A California winter brought crisp blue skies with Cirrus clouds sweeping the expanse like a white whiskbroom. Clifton Brakemeyer and Colonel Schmidt worked the early morning hours poking in and around the blown containers staged in Section B25-26 of the Outer Harbor Terminal's quay yard. As they worked, Stevedores scurried about unloading the container ship Achelois via the huge overhead container cranes, straddle carriers, wheel loaders, yard dogs, and truckers moving containers from the yard to points around the Western U.S.

After two hours of careful inspection of all the exploded containers, Clif and Ada emerged from the black interior of the last container and removed their dust masks.

"If the same bomber blew up the containers and the retail stores of Global International, a different method was used for each," Ada said.

Clif replied, "These containers met their death without fire whereas the retail stores burned like a California forest."

"An accelerant simply wasn't needed in the confined space of each container. The purpose appeared to be the destruction of the Global inventory not the burning of the cargo ship."

"My team did their inspection yesterday afternoon," Clif said. "They took samples of the black dust coating the container interiors, photos, and scans. They sent everything to B-Delta's warehouse in Reno. When our doctor slash forensic pathologist finishes his examination, he'll call me with the results. Now it is time to head to the Sloughhouse Post Office."

The pair of sleuths took Clif's Corvette and blazed east on Interstate 80 to Sacramento and then a series of boulevards, roads, and drives past the community of Sloughhouse to Rancho Murieta and the Sloughhouse Post Office. They parked in the shade of tall evergreens. Lunch hour passed two hours ago so the pair assumed they would be able to talk briefly with the Postmaster.

"My name is Clifton Brakemeyer of B-Delta Security and this is Colonel Ada Schmidt also a consultant to B-Delta. May we have a moment to discuss an important matter regarding letters mailed from this post office?"

The name on the postal worker's tag was Marge. She said, "The FBI was here making asses of themselves a couple of days ago. Something about a letter from here that killed a man in prison. Why don't you talk to them?"

"Are you the Postmaster?" Ada asked nicely.

"No, but I will call him and see if he has time for you."

As no other postal customers occupied the service area, Marge left her window and dodged her way around tables to a small office in the back of the large room. When she reemerged, she waved at Clif and Ada to pass through the swinging gate and meet her at the Postmaster's door.

"You're lucky," Marge whispered. "He's in a descent mood today. Go on in."

Jim Milankovitch, Postmaster of the Sloughhouse Post Office, continued to read a large manual while simultaneously waving his unknown guests into the two chairs opposite his desk. He looked up to analyze the visitors that pursued the letter that brought the FBI to his office.

"Credentials please."

Clif and Ada brought forth their I.D.'s. Ada included her temporary B-Delta Security business card, her German BND identification, and her Nevada driver's license.

The Postmaster spent several minutes on Ada's information after casting long gazes up and down her chassis. He puzzled over her German Intelligence I.D. for at least two minutes.

"What the hell is Bund . . . na . . . chricht . . . endienst?" he asked.

Ada replied, "German Intelligence Service, similar to your FBI. I am a retired Colonel consulting with Mr. Brakemeyer on letters connected to death threats and the actual murder of a man about to be released from prison."

Clif retrieved a selection of photos from his shoulder bag. He handed them over to the Postmaster.

"You will notice that each envelope is addressed to a different person; each envelope has the Sloughhouse postmark canceling the stamp."

He studied them carefully. Jim finally looked up as he tossed the photos in Brakemeyer's direction.

"These are total bullshit," he said.

Clif said, "Why bullshit? How can they be?"

The Postmaster harrumphed as though he spoke to a five-year-old. "You see the dates in the middle of the Sloughhouse cancellation stamp?"

Ada and Clif both said, "Yes."

Jim pointed at the photo on top and said, "On this date our post office was not even open. That's a postal holiday."

He swiped the photo away and pointed at the second. "No mail was canceled on this date or the other two. You see, to get a letter canceled with a Sloughhouse cancellation stamp, a customer *must ask for it*. The mail that passes through this building is sent unaltered to Sacramento for cancelling and distribution to wherever. If a customer specifically asks us to cancel their letter with the Sloughhouse cancellation stamp, its usually for the historic nature of the Sloughhouse Community."

Clif asked, "How do you know someone didn't come in here on these dates and ask for their letter to be canceled here rather than Sacramento?"

The Postmaster harrumphed again and said, "Marge and I know everyone that picks up or drops off mail in this location. If a stranger came in here asking for a Sloughhouse cancellation on their stamp, she or I would remember him or her. Hold on a second."

Jim stepped from his office and hollered at Marge. She turned and scurried to his office.

"Marge," Jim said, "look at these photos and tell me if you remember anyone asking for our cancellation stamp on the dates showing."

The attentive clerk examined the photos. She immediately said, "This one was a holiday, so that is very odd. These others are mid-week when business is slow. I don't remember anyone asking for a stamp cancellation on these dates. We get maybe one or two requests per month – a few more around Christmas. I always know the people."

Brakemeyer looked at the Postmaster and said, "Looks like we have a forger on our hands. Someone copied your stamp. They set the date, canceled the stamp, and then dropped it in the mail, probably at the central hub in Sacramento."

"Copying the stamp is illegal, misdemeanor illegal but still illegal. I don't suppose a forger is outside the realm of possibility. I don't see any other explanation. Are we done here? Marge and I need to return to our *paid* responsibilities."

Clif and Ada took the hint. Clif returned the photos to his satchel. He and Ada thanked both Marge and Jim for their help. Clif left the Postmaster with his business card, and then strolled out of the Post Office.

As they reached the Vette, Ada said, "Let's discuss what we know. You, Cal, Beverly Wells, Gordon Wicks, and Robert Blevins are the people that actively brought down the Defenders of Jasoom."

As the two detectives climbed down into the street-legal racecar, Clif said, "That is correct. So, what's your point?"

"What do we know about the members of this gang that are still alive, but avoided prosecution for conspiracy?"

Clif fired up the Vette and pulled into evening traffic for the ride back to Jack London Square. Ada allowed her partner to think.

The Vette whined and hummed while the traffic whooshed. Finally, Clif said, "Other than their names on a list, and criminal acts committed by the group, we know nothing. God almighty, every member still living is buried in a foreign country behind a medieval wall of protection."

Before Ada could respond, Clif's cell phone rang. He answered hands-free.

"Brakemeyer here."

"Brakemeyer this is Gordon Wicks. Earlier today, I received a letter like the ones you told me about. A number ten envelope in parchment with the Sloughhouse cancellation over the stamp."

"You didn't open it did you?"

Wicks said, "Me open it? Of course not. I had someone else open it."

Clif glanced at Ada. She shook her head in amazement. He said, “So what did the letter say? Are you going to die soon like all the others?”

“I’ll read it to you.”

“No, I’d rather have you take a photo of the letter and email it to me.”

“You really know how to kill my mood, Brakemeyer.”

Wicks signed off. Clif said to Ada, “I really hate that guy. He has all the compassion of a hyena.”

Surprisingly, his cell phone sounded its incoming email sound. Ada picked the phone off its holder and examined the photo of the Sloughhouse letter sent to Wicks. Her eyebrows lifted as she read the message.

“Don’t keep it a secret Colonel,” Clif said.

Ada read, “Because of your duplicitous treachery and greed, there is a bullet coming your way with your name on it. The antiquities black market was never your quick buck industry. You meddled and muddled serious work.”

Clif asked, “No Sun Tzu quote?”

Ada replied, "It closes with a Sun Tzu quote: '*The supreme art of war is to subdue the enemy without fighting. Sun Tzu.*'"

"All right," Clif said. "I've had enough of this crap. These letters are a trap of some kind. Someone is playing with me to see if I'm smart enough to figure out how the mastermind is going to kill me and the other targets involved with the Defenders of Jasoom."

Ada said, "Wicks added a postscript. It reads: Brakemeyer, there is an expression occasionally found on T-shirts and hoodies that reads *Don't piss off old people – the older we get the less 'life in prison' is a deterrent.*' I'm already in prison for the rest of my life. I don't like being bullied or threatened. Whatever I may do to help you find this killer, let me know."

Clif said, "That is interesting. An old delta dog is helping a younger delta dog. Please text him 'message received. I'll be in touch.'"

Ada sent the text, and then allowed herself to think aloud. She said, "The Hindi gallery owner who shot Frederick Mahler is dead. The business belonging to Julia Delmar operated by Robert Blevins is damaged, perhaps irreparably. A weak attempt to land you in jail failed to work. Now, Beverly Wells and Gordon Wicks are marked for murder. Calvin Chu and you are still targets. The mastermind, as you called the killer, is clearly a part of the Defenders of Jasoom. You, Cal, Wicks, and Beverly are targets for revenge. You are being teased into making a mistake. The perpetrator is very afraid of you – or a better way to express it would be *very circumspect about your skills as a detective*."

The miles zipped by as Clif pushed his Vette to excessive speeds. He asked Colonel Schmidt, "How many different ways are there to analyze these letters?"

Ada replied, "Fingerprints are a start. Paper type and origin comes next."

Clif said, "We already performed those tests with no results."

"I don't suppose it would hurt to examine the text and determine the computer program used to create these letters," Ada said thoughtfully. "Maybe there is a language cue like the spelling difference between certain American and British words."

"Yes, I like that thought. We say aluminum while the British say aluminium. We say apartment; the British say flat. We say elevator and they say lift."

"Friend – mate, trunk – boot, vacation – holiday. You've got the idea," Ada said.

"You refer to word processing programs like Office Word, or Corel WordPerfect?"

"Exactly," Ada added. "Freeware word processing programs are also possibilities. There are dozens of them."

"I'm not sure how a word processing program can hide a message. I'll check with Cal," Brakemeyer said. "He has a niece that is a graphic designer for an ad agency in San Francisco – Q&A Solutions Advertising. Her name is Li Xiu I believe."

"Divide and conquer," Ada said.

"I'll track down the obscure members of the Defenders of Jasoom that I missed on my first round of calls. You should retrieve the letters from Hank at the warehouse in Reno, and take them to Li Xiu. I'll have Cal text to you her phone and address. Also, I'm certain Nick would love to see you, even if only for a short visit."

Colonel Schmidt smiled and said, “Understood. I’ll head to Reno early tomorrow. I could use some sleep tonight. There’s nothing better than being rocked to sleep on a boat.”

Clif wished Ada could communicate that sentiment to Gaby. He suddenly remembered he forgot to send flowers to his Swiss Miss. Shit.

***

The merchant of revenge folded the letter and placed it in an envelope addressed to Acucena Cascalho, Rua Jackson Figueiredo Joá, Rio de Janeiro. Snail mail seemed an outdated method of communication but the 13-hour flight from LA to Rio de Janeiro meant the letter would reach its recipient in three days.

Postal mail served its purpose as it related to the deaths of enemies. Besides, the message of death required gamesmanship. This game did not need to be hurried. There was plenty of time to make them sweat. Cena served as the perfect revenge weapon.

She internalized and held hatred like a jackal holds a big meal.

Cena sat at her desk in the office of her Ipanema Galeria. When the queen of zero population growth received her letter, she used a sword-shaped letter opener with gleeful expectation. Without reading it, she placed the letter in her printer and scanned a copy to her office computer. She opened a special program that identified font types.

Cena selected all the text, entered the name of a specific font, and watched the letters pop with a yellow highlight. Stringing the letters together, the message read *Calvin Chu boat Delta Junk berthed slip 12, Oxbow Marina. Destroy when aboard. The opportunity to defeat the enemy is provided by the enemy himself. Sun Tzu.*

The Brazilian beauty opened a new page in her word processing program and began composing a letter to Calvin Chu, 100 Oxbow Marina Drive, Slip #12, Isleton, CA 95641. She filled it with the usual death threats, warnings, and guilt usance.

Laboriously, Cena switched fonts on the letters that spelled out the message she received – *Calvin*

Chu boat Delta Junk berthed slip 12, Oxbow Marina. Destroy when aboard. She placed it in an envelope and addressed it to Wilmer J. Poevinski, 2232 54th Street, Tahoe Park, Sacramento, CA 95820. She then transferred $114,000 in BitCoin to the e-wallet of Mr. Poevinski. A trusted messenger service took the letter to the Correios or Post Office six city blocks east of Cena's Ipanema Galeria.

***

Willy Poe lived in a garage converted into a two-story, one-bedroom apartment. His landlord Mrs. Longacre, a single woman in her seventies, happily accepted his cash rent payments and enjoyed his quiet nature. He never entertained friends, played loud music, or tried to rebuild his old van in her driveway. He did travel a lot. The only mail he received arrived randomly to the apartment's wall-mounted mailbox. A 9x10 manila envelope showed its presence by protruding slightly from the undersized black mail drop.

Willy pulled into the driveway as Mrs. Longacre exited her front door to water her flowers. The day wore a little more heat than usual. The early blooming bulbs like tulips, daffodils, and paper whites needed a drink every few days to stay healthy and happy.

"Hello Mr. Poevinski. You've got mail," Mrs. Longacre said merrily.

Willy slammed his van door as he exited the driver's seat. "Have you been snooping in my mail?" he shouted angrily.

"Oh no, Mr. Poevinski. I would never do that," the old woman said in shock. "I saw it sticking up out of your mail box. That's all I meant."

She dropped her garden hose and turned back to the front door. Willy instantly turned off his suspicion and anger.

He smiled and said, "I apologize Mrs. Longacre. I had no cause to snap at you. I just finished a very tough weight lifting workout at my gym. My mail is from a very special friend, and I didn't get much sleep last night."

The elderly landlord gave Willy a sideways glance of suspicion and said, "That's quite alright Mr. Poevinski." She hustled into her house, closed, and locked the door. For the first time, her tenant showed his threatening dark side; she didn't like it.

The big, gay assassin retrieved the envelope from the mailbox. He carried it, along with a plastic bag holding a new ream of parchment paper and matching #10 envelopes purchased from Office Depot. As he reached his desk, Willy pulled his cell phone and checked his e-wallet. He smiled seeing another $114,000 (two BitCoins) in his BlockCard Bank Account. Cena taught him about cryptocurrencies - and how to use them. His income and wealth left no trace that the Feds could follow. His value in digital money grew nicely.

The big man turned on his laptop and brought up the program that identified fonts. He scanned in the letter from Cena and loaded the parchment stock into the printer. He looked almost comical as he placed a pair of black, horn-rimmed glasses on his face. His right eye needed a small amount of correction. His left eye needed major correction ever since

Clifton Brakemeyer almost ripped it out of his head. He prayed the letter would call for the death of Brakemeyer.

Calvin Chu boat Delta Junk berthed slip 12, Oxbow Marina. Destroy when aboard. Willy read the message and felt a small disappointment. Chu held a partnership with Brakemeyer. The Chinese detective should have died when Niles Ramey threw him naked into the truck with the insects. Brakemeyer saved him. His second time to die had arrived. To fulfill the letter's orders and earn his two BitCoins, he needed to make a bomb. Attached to Calvin Chu's yacht at the water line, at night, a properly designed bomb would explode up and take the detective with it.

Willy used the internet to research Oxbow Marina. He examined several photos of the marina. The boats under cover sat amidst a necklace of tightly packed houses, side-to-side, and back-to-back, with docks on the river. From Tyler Island Road, he could not see the boats in the covered births.

The assassin decided a reconnaissance mission was called for. In the meantime, he created a letter for Calvin Chu. After he completed the message from

Cena word for word, he laboriously substituted the font that would alert the detective to his misfortune. Willy smiled knowing the letter's recipient would never decode the warning. The game of letter and death with hidden codes, poisons, and bombs drove his purpose in life. He thought Cena a genius for constructing the game. Willy had no idea she was only the intermediator.

The harbinger of murder printed the letter, and the properly addressed envelope. He stuck the postage stamp in the envelope corner, and then canceled it with the Sloughhouse Post Office cancellation stamp. He smiled again at the clue no one had figured out. His mistake took the form of assuming no one would.

***

Ada retrieved the letters from the Reno warehouse and then spent the day and night with her significant other, Nick Falkenrath. The next day she performed a power drive to San Francisco where she negotiated the craziness of streets around Fisherman's Wharf.

She parked her Mustang near Pier 35 and hiked the remaining distance to the concrete office building across the tourist-choked lanes. As she announced herself and appointment with Li Xiu to the receptionist, the President and owner of Q&A Advertising appeared by her side.

"My name is Web Arrowsmith," he said affably. "You are here to see Li?"

Ada examined the man in his mid-40's. Web Arrowsmith, a six-foot, two-inch advertising president maintained a solid physique beneath tailored shirts. His broad shoulders and narrow waist caused meaningful glances from both women and men. His thick, wavy brown hair, and startling grey-green eyes sat above a pointed nose with slightly flared nostrils giving him a cruel and dangerous look. Almost all women broke into flirtatious giggles when meeting him. He handled such effrontery with confident, diplomatic aplomb.

Colonel Schmidt did not react in the usual flirtatious manner. With a cool confidence, she shook his hand.

"I am Colonel Ada Schmidt, retired. Nice to meet you. I am working with the B-Delta Security Company investigating the explosions that occurred on the big container ship and Global International retail stores. Detective Calvin Chu's niece Li Xiu may be able to examine and discover some clues relative to letters sent to the victims. She is your graphic artist of some repute I believe."

"Yes," Web answered. "Take as much time as you need. Our workload is a little light today. I'll direct you to her office."

After introductions, Li accepted the two letters and a thumb drive that held images of the letters of Ranjeet Bhabananda and Gordon Wicks. She loaded the images and scanned the other three with her large format scanner.

As Li examined the letters on her two large monitors, Web couldn't hold his curiosity. "What is the story behind these letters Colonel? Unless you can't talk about it for security reasons."

Ada replied, "The first letter was sent to Ranjeet Bhabananda in the California City Correctional Facility southeast of Bakersfield. It contained poison that killed the man almost instantly. The second letter to Beverly Wells held only death threats, as did the fifth to Gordon Wicks, also in prison. The letter to Global International's CEO, Robert Blevins, contained threats of destruction. Four shipping containers with his inventory of furniture and curios from Asia blew up just as the boat passed under the Golden Gate. The fourth letter attempted to indict my boss, Clifton Brakemeyer, with murder. The letter was sent to the San Francisco City Police Department. The only thing in common among them is the paper, and the cancellation stamp from the Sloughhouse Post Office. We believe the stamp is a fake, having queried the Postmaster there."

"Did you say *Sloughhouse?"* Li asked.

"Yes. Sloughhouse is a historic community near Rancho Murieta south of Sacramento. Are you familiar with it?" Ada asked.

"Not the community, but the typeface – the font Sloughhouse. I don't know much about it," Li said, "because it is one of those obscure fonts that faded from use because it looked too much like Times Roman. I think I used it a few times in college and when I first started work here. It's such a cool sounding name."

Web asked Ada, "Why would the letter creator mix fonts that look almost exactly alike?"

Ada became excited. She said, "Because they are hiding a message."

She turned to Li and asked, "Li, will you check each letter for the Sloughhouse font, and if they are present, string them together to see if they spell out any words?"

"Sure," Li replied. "It might take a while. You two should go have a beer somewhere; come back in about half an hour."

Web smiled at Colonel Schmidt. The Buena Vista Café is very close and they have an excellent beer selection. You're German, right? You have to love beer. Also, the Hyde Street Cable Car lends a great deal of clangy ambiance."

Ada replied, "Clangy? Did you just make up that word or is that another American colloquialism?"

"I made it up," Web said.

Ada laughed and said, "I speak German, English, French, Italian, Polish, and Russian. I have to say Americans and British use more silly words than any other country."

Webs said, "Then let's go. We are wasting valuable beer time. The Buena Vista has a Münchner with your name on it."

When the pair returned to check on Li Xiu 45 minutes later, the young graphic designer almost shouted her findings. She waved them to hurry to her workstation.

Li said, "Someone is very clever and very horrible."

"In what way, "Ada asked.

Li held three sheets of paper in her hands. "Well, all but one letter has the Sloughhouse font embedded in the text. The letter to the poisoned man contained the following message in Sloughhouse - *kill with poison dust in letter.* The message to Beverly Wells read - *kill with toxins on car door handle.* The message to Robert Blevins read – *destroy with bombs cargo containers and four stores.* The message to the

San Francisco Police read – *Sam Lion, Clifton Brakemeyer killed Roberto Spawn on his boat and dumped him in the bay near Alcatraz. Include details. Appear weak when you are strong and strong when you are weak.*

Sun Tzu"

"What about the Wicks letter?" Ada asked.

Li shook her head and replied, "I couldn't find any Sloughhouse script in his letter."

Colonel Schmidt turned to Web and asked, "May I borrow Li a bit longer? I need her to highlight the Sloughhouse font on the three letters and print them out. That way any future letters received will be easier for us to find and read the message in Sloughhouse."

Li Xiu said, "I already placed a yellow highlight on the letters in the Sloughhouse font. I'll print them out for you – only take a minute."

Colonel Schmidt turned to Web Arrowsmith and said, "Please excuse me. I need to call the boss immediately."

Web nodded agreement. Ada pulled her cell phone and tapped in Clif Brakemeyer.

"What's up Colonel?" Brakemeyer asked.

"Li Xiu found hidden messages inside almost all the letters. The Sloughhouse cancellation stamp turned out to be the clue."

"How so?" Clif asked.

"The letters were typeset with a font called Times Roman. It's a very common font used for reading because it is easy to read. However, interspersed with the Times Roman text was letters from a typeface called Sloughhouse. Those Sloughhouse letters spelled out messages instructing the sender on how to kill the letter recipient. I'm guessing here, but I think the creator sends out the kill order in some manner like email, text message, or postal mail. The assassin resends the letter with the Sloughhouse cancellation stamp and the coded message as a joke on Brakemeyer and Chu."

"What did the messages say?" Clif asked.

"The most important message was in the Beverly Wells letter. I say this because she has not yet been killed. The Sloughhouse message read - *kill with toxins on car door handle.*"

“Oh, holy hell,” Clif said. “I’ll call Bev and Cal immediately and let them know to avoid the danger. Good work Colonel. Ah, you said *almost* all the letters.”

“The letter to Gordon Wicks contained no Sloughhouse fonts. Its composition only showed Times Roman.”

“Is someone trying to point a finger at Wicks or is he the mastermind behind these killings and corporate destructions?”

Colonel Schmidt said, “I do not know. The game someone is playing just got more complex and more dangerous.”

“Agreed,” Clif said. “Are you willing to see this gambit through Colonel? I don’t want you to become collateral damage when the hit is put on me or Cal.”

Ada replied quickly and firmly. “I believe you still need my help. I am in. What next?”

“Meet me at the boat,” Clif ordered. “I’ll make my calls to Cal and Bev, and ask Cal to head for the Lujon. We need a three-way strategy session and a briefing for my security team.”

“Roger that,” Ada said.

Web Arrowsmith stepped up to Colonel Schmidt and said, “Excuse me for eavesdropping, but I was going to ask you to have dinner with me and my wife Archie. Based upon your comments to your boss, I’d say you are going to be busy.”

“You are correct,” Ada said. “I have a meeting with both my bosses as soon as I reach the office. Thank you anyway.”

“Rain check, Colonel?”

“Certainly, if I may bring my fiancé.”

“By all means,” Web said effusively. “Our dining room has the best view in the bay area.”

Six
The Sixth Letter

Willy Poe mailed Calvin Chu's letter. Waiting to execute the kill order required time for the man to receive the letter and read it. While he waited, he would place the bomb on Chu's boat with a trigger sensor designed to detonate when Chu climbed aboard. If he hadn't read the letter yet, so what he thought. He could then perform the kill order on Beverly Wells, which was long overdue.

The man did not mind working with plastic explosives. He did not like handling deadly toxins. He rented a 10'x 25' storage shed where his bomb making materials and toxins resided in two bombproof safes. His gas mask and HAZMAT suit nested in a tall, single-door locker. He also kept a sniper rifle, semi-automatic rifle, a 9mm handgun, tactical clothing, and ammunition in a special two-door locker.

A sharps container accepted Willy's used lab-ware like gloves, papers, plastic pipettes and pipette tips, and any other item contacting the toxins. His autoclave used steam heat to neutralize higher molecular weight toxins like the ones he used on Ranjeet Bhabananda.

The poison meister's instructions meant placing toxin powder on the door handle of Beverly Wells' car. The weather forecast included the usual fog blanket over the city between dusk and dawn, but no rain. Rain would wash away or dilute the toxins reducing their effectiveness. One or two applications should do the trick. The journalist still used her car to travel about the city and East Bay.

Willy set to work making the bomb first and toxin cocktail second. A weather front crawled from the ocean across northern California. When night arrived, he donned a wetsuit and headed for Oxbow Marina.

***

Beverly drove a dark blue 2020 model Ford Focus hatchback. She parked it on Stanyan or Fulton Streets, as her three-story apartment building contained no garages. Despite certain drawbacks, Beverly's two-bedroom apartment featured a bay window facing Golden Gate Park. Remodeled with fresh white paint, hardwood floors, and stainless-steel kitchen, Bev's little nest made for a comfortable and semi-safe existence.

Since receiving the call about her car being sabotaged with toxins, Beverly allowed her life to be ruled by a team of security agents from B-Delta. Commander Johnson arranged an invisible stakeout team designed to protect the Wells woman and capture the person placing toxins on her car. Each team member carried a backpack or shoulder bag containing a full-face respirator, clear plastic gloves, and weapons. They dressed in casual clothes geared for 40-degree weather.

Johnson staged himself inside the apartment where he could sit in a bedroom chair and watch the street where Beverly's car awaited a toxin assault. A B-Delta agent staged himself at the corner the St. Ignatius Church on the corner of Parker Avenue and Fulton Street. Another took a position in the trees in Golden Gate Park, kitty-corner from Bev's apartment building. Across Stanyan Street, the final agent hid in the sheltered doorway of an old apartment building resembling a Motel 6.

After a thorough safety check by the security team, Beverly parallel parked her car on Fulton Street rather than Stanyan for surveillance purposes. The B-Delta Team possessed no idea when the killer might strike. Brakemeyer, Chu, and Schmidt briefed the team on what to expect. This person was likely a paid assassin with weapons and fighting skills rather than a Unabomber nerd.

On their second night of deployment, Beverly killed the lights in her apartment and retired to bed. Johnson assumed a position at the bay window. He performed a com check with each of his team members and then watched the shadows for movement.

Streetlights on all four corners of the Stanyan and Fulton intersection made sneaking difficult. At 2 a.m., a large, dark figure ambled up Fulton Street until he entered the brightly lit corner.

"Team, this is Team Leader," Johnson said in a normal tone. Beverly sat up in bed instantly awake and climbing out.

"What's going on?" she asked.

Johnson shushed her and waved her back to bed. He spoke to his com, "We have a bogey approaching the car. Everyone gear up and close in."

Willy Poe had examined the streets from a distance. He tried using a night vision scope but the corner streetlights turned night into a vision of the sun. The toxin assassin believed he had no concerns since no one knew when he might strike. Enough time had passed since he sent Beverly Wells her letter that his enemy's focus must have shifted elsewhere.

Willy took his time strolling across the intersection and angling to the street where he could approach the driver's side door. The four men closing in on him remained hidden.

Suddenly, he thought he heard footsteps. As Willy turned, a snapping sound preceded a large, thick net sweeping over him from his neck down. It wrapped him so tightly he couldn't move his arms. A second net covered and wrapped his head and upper body.

Johnson emerged from the apartment building door. He said to his com, "Pick up the package now."

A new, dark van pulled up and double-parked alongside Beverly's car. Two men jumped from the back doors. They laid down a black body bag and unzipped it.

Willy screamed, "You fuckers! You're all dead. I'm covered in poisons that will kill you in minutes!"

All the B-Delta agents wore full tactical clothing plus dark chemical jumpsuits, gloves, and masks. The professional team shoved a wad of cloth into Willy's mouth through the netting. Duct tape secured it, muffling his curses.

In seconds, Willy found himself zipped inside the bag and loaded into the van. It took four men to load the writhing assassin.

Johnson said, "Take him to the warehouse jail. Leave him with ankle and wrist chains and cuffs. No talking to or discussions with the prisoner. Keep him gagged and bagged until the boss is ready to interrogate him."

***

Dr. May Tockterman met San Francisco City Detective Calvin Chu the night he pursued Willy Poe and the Defenders of Jasoom. She treated Willy's damaged eye and released him from emergency care on Cal's suggestion. Since that time, they dated in a serious fashion.

She had not seen Cal since their angry discussion over his choice of lifestyle and private detective work with Clifton Brakemeyer. May missed the inflexible, intractable detective whose handsome Asian features left her bemused.

She phoned him several times and received his answering message each time. Maybe, she thought, the best way to make amends and reconstitute their relationship involved a personal visit. The doctor of general medicine knew the route to Oxbow Marina and Slip #12. She would drive to the East Bay, Concord, Pittsburgh, Antioch, Rio Vista, and then a few zigzags until she reached Oxbow Marina Drive.

An unusual weather front struck the West Coast. The early spring storm dumped snow in the Sierras and rain in the valley. May would have preferred to stay home on her day off and let the rain sing to her as it bounced off the roof and windows of her house. However, she'd put off meeting Cal long enough. He meant more to her than the drawbacks she once considered *deal killers*.

Doctor Tockterman decided rain or no rain, she would visit Cal at his boat. Despite Cal's answering message saying '*I'm not in right now please leave a message,*' he would arrive eventually. May would wait for him in the cozy confines of his 51' Bluewater Coastal Cruiser.

***

Cal finished the cleanup at Beverly's apartment and parking area. He assured her she would never receive another Sloughhouse letter. The assassin, Willy Poe, held information that would expose the other players in the game. Willy would give up that intel and then learn to swim in the ocean around the shark-infested Farallon Islands.

Despite his wish to spend more time with Beverly, he felt compelled to return to the Lujon to meet with Johnson and the other team members for a debrief of their mission the previous night.

In his jail cell at the B-Delta Security warehouse in Reno, Willy remained wrapped in netting and tightly zipped inside the black body bag. He could breathe through a small opening near the top of the zipper above his head. The toxins intended for Beverly Wells' car remained inside a carefully constructed squeeze bulb with *inflow and outflow* tubes. His right hand, strapped to his side by the netting, lay inches from the delivery tube in his jumpsuit pocket. As long as no one dropped him on his side or conveyed a hard blow to the area, he would be safe.

"Hello Willy," the familiar voice said.

The man in the bag recognized Brakemeyer's voice. Fury brought wriggling and muffled curses as the big man failed to control his rage.

"Willy, you must calm down before we may carry on a reasonable conversation."

Several minutes passed before the captive relaxed and appeared ready to converse. He managed to bend his head enough to nod a *yes* motion through the bag.

Brakemeyer unzipped the bag and examined the netting confines keeping the killer in check. The *net guns* did a marvelous job of wrapping the man like a butterfly worm in a cocoon.

"Willy," Brakemeyer began, "I shall remove the tape gag so you may speak. I will not release you from your bonds or shackles until you answer my questions truthfully. Do you understand?"

Willy's eyes conveyed a rage and asperity that Brakemeyer understood. The prisoner drew air through his nose in volumes designed to calm his breathing and anger. He finally locked eyes with his enemy and nodded in the affirmative.

Brakemeyer reached down and ripped the duct tape gag from Willy's face. The trussed assassin drew another large breath through his mouth.

"You will release me Mr. Detective," Willy said. "And when you do, I will spend the rest of my life, my resources, and my skills hunting you down and killing you in a very nasty way."

"Feel better now Mr. Poe?" Brakemeyer asked. "My bottom line is an exchange – answers to my questions for your life and a chance to kill me just like you said. You've been playing a game with me so now I will play this game with you. All you have to do is trust me to keep my end of my bargain, and tell me what I want to know."

"I'm not going to tell you jack-shit," Willy snarled.

"Then you will never get out of those nets my friend. I'll leave you to die of thirst and starvation, covered in your own excrement, right where you lay. After you're dead, I'll drive into the most remote part of the Nevada high desert and bury you deep. I don't suppose anyone will miss you; due process is not in your horoscope. I'll give you time to think about it while I go have lunch with some friends of mine."

Clif found a location on Willy's wrist where he could shoot a hypodermic needle into a vein through the netting. The solution contained a powerful mixture of truth serums including sodium pentothal, scopolamine, and sodium thiopental.

Brakemeyer's lunch with Ada and Nick Falkenrath, re-energized his good mood. He felt light, buoyant, and ready to deal with his captive killer.

He returned to the warehouse and entered his prisoner's cell. He launched into his interrogation.

"Well, Willy," the owner of B-Delta Security said, "I'm glad to see you didn't go anywhere."

The prisoner cried uncontrollably. When Brakemeyer spoke to him, his eyes bugged out and he began laughing and foaming at the mouth. His state of agitation wasn't conducive to answering questions.

Brakemeyer left the cell and returned with a bucket of water. Willy lapsed into a moaning dementia until the jail keeper dumped the cold water on his face. The big prisoner coughed and sputtered like an engine running out of gas.

"That's better Willy," Brakemeyer said. "I really hate keeping you tied up and bagged up. I could release you and let you take a shower, eat some hot food, and drink all the water you'd like. Wouldn't you rather answer my questions, Willy?"

"I just want to rip your eyes out and kill you like you killed Roberto and Niles."

"Hey, you're back from the delirium," Brakemeyer said. "You know Willy, I don't think you could kill me the way I killed your two friends. Roberto took a kick to the face, fell into the bay, and drowned in the middle of the night. Niles . . . well I broke his knee, I used a shotgun to blow away his shoulder and hip, and then I let the Tsetse flies and disease-laced mosquitos feast on him. The insects crawled in and out of his mouth as he screamed. I didn't have time to enjoy the sight as I had to save Detective Chu."

Willy laughed and said, "You can't save him this time you piece of shit. He's a *dead man walking*."

Brakemeyer pulled his cell phone and called Cal. When he answered Clif said, "Cal, check for bombs on your car, your boat, even the Lujon. Poe says you're a dead man walking. He put something in place like toxins or a bomb that doesn't need his attendance to work."

Cal replied, "Got it, Clif. I'll enlist Johnson and team to help me search."

Brakemeyer signed off and felt relief. Beverly avoided toxin death and Cal a similar toxin or bombing death. He turned to the creature on the floor.

"Willy, Calvin Chu is just fine. I've alerted him to your threat. So, let's get back to my questions and your answers. Brakemeyer took his time and slowly broke down Willy's resolve. The mumbled answers included where he lived, a vague description of his rental storage unit, and achieving revenge on the people that killed the leaders of the Defenders of Jasoom.

"Willy," Brakemeyer said gently, "I have to assume that Acucena Cascalho is either your contact or the mastermind behind these letters. I'm certain I'll find evidence in your apartment, but why don't you tell me about Acucena."

Willy grumbled, "Her name is Cena you asshole. Cena is the most wonderful person I know. Her personal body guard trained me, and Cena made me rich."

"Where is she Willy? Still in Brazil at her gallery?"

"It's the Ipanema Galeria, you idiot."

"You say her personal body guard trained you. Does Cena have other guards?"

"Of course she does," Willy rasped. "She's rich and keeps ex-military around to protect her. Two travels with her at all times and six cover her home in rotation with six others."

"Willy, why did the Sloughhouse letter you sent to Gordon Wicks have no message coded in the font Sloughhouse?"

"How the hell should I know?" Willy said. "Cena sends me the letters with the message coded in. I make a new one with the coded message, stamp it, and send it. The letter to Wicks had no code."

"Was Cena saving me for the last target?"

"She never told me, but process of elimination Mr. Genius. She still refers to you as Sam Lion."

"Last question, Willy. What did you do to kill Calvin Chu?"

"I made a bomb with a motion sensor."

"Where did you place the bomb?"

"On his boat, of course. It's just below the waterline under the boarding ramp from the dock. As soon as he steps on board and the boat rocks – boom!"

Willy laughed but Brakemeyer did not.

***

Cal purposely left May Tockterman's call messages, emails, and texts unanswered. His attitude ran along the lines of *she dumped me for no good reason so to heck with her.*

Receiving Brakemeyer's call about a potential bomb or toxin attack, and then a second call telling him the bomb was on the waterline of the Delta Junk. Now, panic swam up his spine. A foreboding piled onto the panic like he left the door to Fort Knox open, or he walked naked through the girl's dorm at Wellesley.

Cal searched his phone for the most recent contact from May. She called this morning and left a message. He listened to it in horror.

"Cal, this is May. I really wish to talk with you and apologize for my attitude that removed me from your life. I desperately need to see you again. I'm heading for your boat where I will wait for you until you come home. All my love."

Cal did a *call back* to May's phone but she did not answer. He left a voice message to *stay away from his boat.* He placed his second call to the Oxbow Marina Yacht Club Office. There was no answer. He left a similar message on their phone. He next called the Isleton Police Department. Officer Beaks answered.

Cal attempted a calm voice but failed. "Has there been an incident at the Oxbow Marina?"

"Not that we are aware. Who is this? Who is calling?"

"My name is Calvin Chu, Detective for the San Francisco City Police retired. I received information about a bomb being placed on my boat. Please contact the nearest bomb squad and prevent anyone from accessing boats berthed in the covered slips at Oxbow Marina. My boat is the Delta Junk in Slip #12. I tried calling the Yacht Club but only the answering machine took my call. Please call the Oxbow Manager's office. I am in Oakland right now, heading for Oxbow as soon as I reach my car."

Cal hung up. Johnson and the team were given two days off before training sessions began again. The panic-stricken detective raced off the boat and to his SUV. The windy wetness of a dark, rainy day struck his face like birdshot fired from a rifle. If he pushed his Expedition and violated several traffic laws, he could reduce the one-hour drive to 45 minutes.

As Cal drove like a qualifier for the Indy 500, his wiper blades on the fastest setting could barely keep up with the downpour. He used the hands-free voice to call May every few minutes.

Cal crossed the toll bridge over the San Joáquin River in a fury that stopping to pay the toll should slow him down. The flat ag land he raced across lay mostly below the level of the Sacramento and San Joáquin River.

Just before reaching the Brannan Island State Park, he saw a smoke pillar rising in the general direction of Oxbow Marina. His heart leaped to his throat. He called May for the fifteenth time.

"Hello Mr. Calvin Chu," May said brightly. "It's about time you called."

Cal shouted, "Oh thank god, May. You are alright. Where are you?"

"I'm on your boat waiting with a big surprise for you."

The distraught detective said, "You are on the Delta Junk, my boat?"

"Yes," May said. "Am I in trouble? I called for you but got no answer so I sort of snuck on board. I just wanted to surprise you."

Cal yelled at his phone, "May, please sit quietly and don't move an inch. There is a bomb attached to my boat at the water line below the gangway. It should have detonated when you crossed the gangway and stepped on the boat. Either the bomb builder set his sensor for a lateral motion instead of a vertical one or the trigger is less sensitive than planned. Anyway, don't move. I'm only a few minutes out."

May grew both concerned and angry. “Are you qualified to defuse a bomb? You stay away from here until a bomb expert shows up.”

Cal said with some heat of his own, “I’ve not been able to reach anyone in the Yacht Club or manager’s office. The Isleton Police are notified but that’s it for the moment. If someone in the marina decides to move their boat a little too fast, the bomb could be set off. Keep your phone on so I can talk to you. Do not move.”

The monsoon lightened to a sprinkle as the miles flew by. Cal chased an egret off the road as he barreled across highway 12 from Isleton to Oxbow. The smoke he saw became a farmer burning the last of his detritus before burning season ended. The wet atmosphere turned his burning into a smoky mess.

As Cal turned onto Oxbow Marina Drive, he spotted the flashing lights of a single police car. Detective Chu turned into the Marina complex and drove to a parking area opposite the covered berths containing Slip #12. He jumped out and ran for the gangway connecting the parking area with the covered berths.

An Isleton Police Officer stepped in front of him. "Hold it buddy," he said. "I can't let you go in there. We got word a bomb may be on one of the boats."

"I know," Cal said panting. "I called it in. My name is Detective Calvin Chu of the San Francisco City Police Department – retired. I live on the boat in Slip #12. My girlfriend walked on board a while ago and did not set off the bomb. It has a motion sensor switch."

"And how do you know that?" the skeptical officer asked.

Cal replied, "I choose not to answer that question. Let's just say my sources are 100% accurate. I am part owner of B-Delta Security LLC. We offer services including private security, risk management, advice and training, and support for law enforcement, multinational corporations, and prominent individuals. Clifton Brakemeyer is the President and CEO."

"That name sounds familiar," the officer said. "Listen, I have members of the Oakland bomb squad flying in by chopper. They should be here in less than twenty minutes. Are you in touch with your girlfriend on the boat?"

"Yes," Cal said.

"Call her and let me talk to her."

Cal did as the officer requested. "May, listen to me. Officer Hanks of the Isleton Police would like to speak with you."

The detective handed the phone to the officer. "Hello, Dr. Tockterman, this is Officer Hanks. It looks as though you wandered into a very dangerous situation. I managed to convince the Oakland Bomb Squad to fly up here and defuse this bomb and dispose of it. Please remain calm and unmoving. We will work to keep the water calm and prevent anyone from venturing into or out of the marina. Understood?"

Officer Hanks handed the phone back to Detective Chu. "She wants to talk to you."

As Cal took the phone, the Rio Vista Police Department and fire trucks from the Isleton Volunteer Fire Department and the Rio Vista Fire Department arrived with sirens honking and lights flashing.

Cal and Officer Hanks found themselves quickly surrounded by police and firefighters demanding to know the situation. Cal told May to wait and stay still. He would call her back in a few minutes.

Rain diminished to mist as Officer Hanks filled in the first responders with Cal adding important details. The men and women spread themselves to all ingress points from the main parking lot to the last gangway, providing access to the covered berths. They prevented all boat owners from moving their watercrafts until the crisis ended.

That's when children, from a small palm tree-covered park facing the interior waters of the marina directly across from Slip #12, began throwing stones into the water. They yelled with excitement at the flashing lights of the fire and rescue trucks. They ran about grabbing anything available to toss into the water.

Officer Hanks spotted the kids, jumped in his car, and sped around the doublewide trailer homes and pre-manufactured homes lining the interior of the marina. When he arrived at the cul-de-sac, he yelled at the children to stop throwing things into the water. The well-behaved children, with respect for authority, began throwing stones at Officer Hanks.

The largest of the youngsters, probably a 13 or 14-year-old boy, picked up a small boulder a foot wide, and shot put it into the water. The splash pushed waves in perfect circles toward the boats under the covered berths. The distance of 100 feet dropped the ring wave heights to almost nothing, but the calm water amplified the combination of rings from all the stones thrown in.

Everyone watched in horror as the outer ring ripple pushed a mini-tsunami wave ahead of it. The slight rise in the water as it passed through the berths should not have been enough movement to set off the bomb.

The explosion blew the Delta Junk in half and sank it. The orange mushroom cloud blasted through the roof of the dock canopy. The shock wave crushed the boats on either side and opposite the Delta Junk. Most of the dock running between the moored boats shredded and sank. The boats that did not sink pushed into each other, listing badly.

The rock-tossing boys and all persons standing within a radius of 1,800 feet found themselves knocked to the ground and unconscious. Cal and two firefighters were blown into the trees lining the divider between Oxbow Marina Drive and the gangway entrance to the destroyed berths. Houses on both sides of the marina were damaged. The house closest to Slip #12 and the park where the kid threw the final stone only contained half its original shape. Gas lines ruptured and fires burst into a conflagration.

Firefighters from the Rio Vista Fire Department accidentally found shelter behind their trucks. The moment they recovered from the shock, they jumped in their fire trucks and drove around the marina where they hooked up their hoses to a fire hydrant and began shooting water onto the burning house and its neighbors.

People injured by flying glass and projectiles wandered outside their homes and phoned for first responders that were already present. As the minutes, and hours passed, ambulances arrived from Lodi, Walnut Grove, and Stockton.

Cal regained consciousness in the California Urgent Care facility on Kettleman Lane, Lodi. His saline I.V. drip washed painkillers into his system and kept the concussion victim hydrated.

In his most lucid manner, the homeless man asked his nurse if he might make a cell phone call to his friend. She brought him his phone.

"Mr. Chu, you are suffering from shock and a severe concussion. Please do not become too excited or upset."

She handed him the phone. Cal said, "Define too excited."

The caring nurse said, "You know what I mean. If your blood pressure goes through the roof, you won't get any more phone calls or visitors for quite a while."

Cal said, "Thank you nurse. I'll do my best to remain calm, but it won't be easy."

He dialed Clif Brakemeyer. "Cal, you're awake," Clif said. "How are you feeling?"

"I just woke up. What's the latest on everything?"

"You've been out for nearly five days. You probably figured out the explosion that knocked you 30 feet into a palm tree destroyed your boat, and May I'm afraid. I'm so sorry Cal."

"That fucker Willy Poe hasn't seen the last of me. I want a piece of that son-of-a-bitch."

Brakemeyer said, "Cal, I must apologize yet again. After I heard about what happened at Oxbow, I lost my temper. I rented an Airbus EC 120 Colibri from my friends at Reno Chopper Service. Colonel Schmidt is rated to fly that helicopter so she and I flew that worthless shred of human excrement to the northern most saltpan of the Black Rock Desert Wilderness – about 50 miles north of Gerlach and 40 miles north of the annual Burning Man Festival. Willy is buried six feet, face down, in the midst of white salt and calcium, in the middle of nowhere. He may refloat when the next ice age fills the area with another lake; but I doubt it."

"Take me up there sometime so I may spit on his grave," Cal said still angry. What is next on the agenda?"

"You live and recuperate on the Lujon until the doctors say you are good to go. I'm told two weeks to two months. Beverly has jumped in to help. She's arranging for your medical records to be transferred to a specialist in Oakland upon your release from this fine institution."

"I have no clothes, no mementos, no identity, and no woman."

"Beverly will take you to buy new clothes, shoes, and anything else you may need. She will also help you look for another boat."

"No . . . no more boats. I want a house or apartment in the city. San Francisco is where I belong."

Brakemeyer smiled at his ailing best friend and said, "Whatever you want, Beverly will help you find and implement."

"I need to help you, Clif. I can't just sit around."

"Oh yes you can, and will," Brakemeyer said. "You will recover completely and rebuild your life before we tackle our next project. That's an order partner."

“And what will you do now that our Sloughhouse killer is visiting another universe?”

“Acucena Cascalho sent the letters with instructions to Willy. He carried out her orders. She deServes a reckoning for her actions both with the Defenders of Jasoom and the Sloughhouse Letters. I intend to mail a special Sloughhouse letter to Cena Cascalho. I have a message for her that will darken her world. The reckoning comes after she tells us if anyone above her is pulling strings.”

“Good luck, partner,” Cal said. “I owe you one.”

“You owe me a contented disposition and healthy body. If you lapse into melancholy man, I’ll beat the crap out of you.”

Cal smiled and said, “Not even on your best day, buddy. Best of luck to you and the team.”

Seven
The Search for Answers

Gabriella Uhlmann lived in a small, one-bedroom apartment in Les Muguets, (Lily of the Valley), France. It cost half her monthly salary from Swiss Air, but it was the cheapest place she could find within 10 minutes of Geneva Airport.

Unmarried flight attendants for airlines usually roomed together to save money. Gaby chose not to have roommates fussing over her and her baby to be. She kept her pregnancy a secret. Gaby paced about her apartment worrying. The flowers Brakemeyer sent helped her mood but did not resolve her quandary.

Abortion wasn't an option. Since her brother's tragic death from AIDS a few years prior, death of a loved one brought trepidity by the plane load. Brakemeyer engaged dangerous people in his business. The work didn't frighten him but it scared the future out of Gaby. She might as well be in love with a coal miner.

She could continue to work as a flight attendant for 24 more weeks or longer with a doctor's permission. Being a single mom would be beyond difficult. She earned so little money and the cost of Swiss living left little room for low-income people. Every pilot she knew wore a wedding ring. She wasn't about to attempt the theft of a man from his wife.

The father of her child, Clifton Brakemeyer, represented the love of her life. Gaby could go to him, marry him, and live his lifestyle with a newborn. She knew she would be unhappy and fearful. Of the options in front of her, Clif represented the best choice. If he would not come to her then she would have to go to him. Her resolve to remain in Switzerland weakened. He loved her and she loved him. Maybe the time was right to open a new dialogue with her ex-Navy SEAL, ex-police detective, and ex-boyfriend. What the hell, she thought. Life offered no guarantees. You live it, work through the tough parts, and enjoy the fun parts. At the very least, Clif could buy his wife and daughter a family season pass at the Heavenly Valley Ski Resort.

***

Cena finished swimming laps in her pool. She climbed up the pool steps, pulled a towel from the head of a statue of Romulus. Each pool corner featured a statue of either Romulus or Remus, the mythological founders of the Roman Civilization.

Perched high on a mountain plateau, the domicilio Cascalho overlooked the Atlantic Ocean, Sao Conrado, and the peaks surrounding Gavea and Vidigal. The view from the pool, framed by palm trees and flowering Bougainvillea's, combined misty mountains, blue ocean, white crashing waves on rocky cliffs, and distant skyscrapers hugged by mountains of the Tijuca National Park. Cena owned the empty lot next to her home, but not the monster mansion wedged between her and the cliff.

Cena toweled her hair dry as she performed a smooth climb up the steps to her ultra-modern mansion. Her ever present guards looked at everything accept their boss. The gallery owner heiress drank a glass of mixed fruit juice pre-poured for her by the housekeeper. She showered and changed to a comfortable tropical Jenny before retiring to her in-home office.

Cena reviewed a checklist of action items for her gallery. Her assistant would handle them all. Her focus recently shifted away from her Galeria and toward her revenge objective. Too many days passed since she last contacted Willy Poe. She needed an update on his progress with the Wells woman and Detective Calvin Chu.

The large stack of junk mail on her desk, brought there each day by Alandra the maid, contained a letter in parchment. Cena snatched it noticing the Sloughhouse cancellation stamp. She zipped it open with her sword-shaped letter opener and extracted the 8.5 x 11 sheet with computer-typewritten text. It appeared to be from Willy Poe but something seemed wrong. He'd never communicated with her in this manner before. It read:

Cena - I carried out my orders on the Wells woman, Calvin Chu, and Clifton Brakemeyer. Job done. Please advise any other projects I may help resolve. Does the big boss wish other members of the Defenders of Jasoom eliminated? Again, I am ready and waiting for your contact.

Willy

P.S. Thank you for expanding my BlockCard Bank Account. Retirement is getting closer each day.

The zero-population fanatic dropped the letter and drew a deep breath. Willy Poe would not send her a letter. He would not refer to a *big boss* since he didn't know of anyone giving her instructions. He would not refer to an *expanding* BlockCard account and *retirement.*

Cena scanned the letter into her font recognition program. She highlighted text made with the font Sloughhouse. Reading the message brought an anger she could barely control. It read:

Willy killed Dr. May Tockterman. He failed to kill Cal Chu and Beverly Wells. Willy is dead, and now I am coming for you. Escape is futile. See you soon.

Brakemeyer or Sam Lion if you prefer.

The flush to Cena's cheeks radiated through her lovely caramel skin. Fury guided her fist to her desktop. The crashing sound brought her guards and housekeeper. She dismissed the housekeeper and spoke to the guards.

"Someone is coming to kill me. Find several dozen more guards and alert your friends in the Rio Civil Police. I want them ready to arrest the criminals when they arrive at the airport. The only names I know are Clifton Brakemeyer and Calvin Chu. Brakemeyer may travel under the name Sam Lion. Don't miss any companions. I want this house covered on all three sides with enough fire power to bring down a battalion of Marines."

The commander of the guards said, "Yes mam. Straightaway."

Cena realized that the former artist detective figured out their game. He was attempting to flip the tables on her but he would fail. Brazil was her country. The guards and police were her friends. Her only fear lay in the corruptibility of the PCRJ (Polícia Civil do Rio de Janeiro). She needed to make certain that

Brakemeyer could not influence them with wads of cash.

For the first time since Cena became involved with the Defenders of Jasoom, she felt fear and dread. Her anonymity was blown. Brakemeyer escaped death at the hands of three very qualified killers named Niles T. Ramey, Roberto Spawn, and Willy Poe. All three died by Brakemeyer's hand. Now he was after her.

***

The spring day in Northern Nevada wore windless blue skies. The dirt road diverging from Highway 95 east of Reno appeared the same as a thousand other Nevada dirt roads. Its entrance, protected by a cattle grate and cattle gate, remained closed and pad locked at all times. The dirt road ran straight upslope and disappeared into a ravine between two low peaks.

The mountains in this area of Nevada resembled a piece of paper wadded up and then spread out again. Their rounded ridges and peaks ranged no more than a few thousand feet above the high Nevada desert.

The road wandered the ravines for six miles before it came to a tangent dirt road with yet another cattle gate. This locked gate led to a minor mining operation with a poppet head tower or headframe, and winding house. Nearby, a bunkhouse held up to four dozen people with sleeping, eating, and bathing facilities. On its own flat paddock a few hundred feet away an ore assay building, storage building, and powerhouse with two-80kw diesel powered, four stroke generators, possessed all the elements of a typical mining operation. A helipad of poured concrete was painted with basketball court lines. A 100,000-gallon water tank, supplemented by infrequent rainwater, provided potable and grey water needs for the entire compound. This facility was not what it appeared to be.

Immediately after setting up the warehouse in Reno, Clif Brakemeyer leased 80 acres of remote property from the Bureau of Land Management (BLM), filed a mining claim, and hired a construction company to build the fake mining operation.

From the air or satellite, the facility looked exactly like the typical small Nevada mining operation. In fact, the area served as a private security-training center for B-Delta Security. Rooms attached to the bunkhouse held classrooms, fitness center, weapon displays, and an indoor shooting range.

Brakemeyer's team practiced weapons manipulation, firearms training, and building clearing. A three-story tactical house and sniper tower with a modular wall and air venting system, allowed training for searches, smoke and gas deployments, multi-elevation firearms training, and rappelling.

The team kept fitness as a high priority. Besides the workout room, outside the buildings a PT track tested strength, speed, agility, and stamina.

To lead the team on a mission Ada felt she needed to prove herself worthy. In the classroom, she explained to the team how the BND worked, its different divisions and purposes. Ada recalled many of her operations including those with live fire.

Colonel Schmidt then proceeded to outshoot every member of the team from close, medium, and long-range including sniper fire from 300 yards. She ran the obstacle course in record time, and rappelled down the three-story building with total competence. She earned everyone's respect especially Clifton Brakemeyer's. The man remained impressed that this woman of amazing military talents loved a guy that made furniture.

With everyone in the conference room, Brakemeyer explained the reason for their undertaking. They all knew about the explosions inside the Global International containers, the retail stores, and Calvin Chu's boat. They captured one of the terrorists outside Beverly Wells' apartment. Now they needed to capture the person behind the terror. Acucena Cascalho would be heavily protected by private guards and the Rio de Janeiro Civil Police.

Brakemeyer pointed to a map on the wall projected from a laptop computer's SmartSHOW 3D program. "We will fly into Asuncion, Paraguay. My contacts at the Defion Internacional in Lima will preposition an AgustaWestland AW139 helicopter at the Asuncion International Airport. Their pilot will do the flying from there to a refueling stop in Cornélio Procópio – Francisco Lacerda Junior Airport, Brazil.

After refueling, we fly to a farm in the mountains north of Taubaté. Two SUV's will be prepositioned at the edge of an open field. We drive four hours to Joá. Team A heads to the Ipanema Galeria at Ipanema Beach. Team B heads to Joá and the Cascalho estate. Both teams have taken several classes in Brazilian Portuguese. Keep your translators safely pocketed inside your clothes in case we are surprised by someone."

Colonel Schmidt said, "We are taking this long and complicated route to avoid controlled airspace. The refueling stop in Cornélio Procópio Airport is a minor danger point. Cornélio Procópio is a small isolated town about half way to our target. Our trust in the Defion Private Security Service will be tested. It is their responsibility to bribe the company performing our refueling. The Francisco Lacerda Junior Airport will overlook our illegal entry into Brazil on both refueling stops – into and out of the country. If we are caught, we are on our own. No government bailouts or prisoner exchanges. This operation is very expensive. It is where we earn our money."

Johnson and all the team members kept grim expressions, and a determination mindset that made them the top professionals in their game. They all possessed a passion for dangerous adventure, but they also followed orders endeavoring to keep the mayhem to a minimum. Cowboys were not allowed. Mission success was everything.

Systematically, the private security commandos reviewed each step of their operation. Brakemeyer continue with the briefing.

"At 2:00 a.m., Colonel Schmidt leads Team A to the Ipanema Galeria to raid Cena's office. Surveillance for police comes first. If police are present, they will be neutralized with non-lethals. The team cuts the power to the building at the exterior breaker box, and then breaks in from the alley between the Galeria and the 'L' shaped building surrounding it. Team A will confiscate laptops, CPUs, and files pertaining to any international affairs. Maximum time in the building will be 10 minutes. Escape will be west up the one-way Rua Anibal de Mendonça to the Avenue Epitácio Pessoa. Traveling down the coast to Joá, the team will head for the rendezvous point of Estrada do

Joá and Rua Jackson de Figueiredo. At 2:30 a.m., Team B, led by me, will knock out the power transformers shutting down electricity to the residential area around Acucena Cascalho's estate. The balance of the team will disperse from the tree cover on the street below the mansion's swimming pool. Night vision glasses will enable the team to spot guards moving. Johnson will carry a thermal telescopic body heat detector. Each team member carries a set of lethal weapons including handguns, smoke grenades, and hand grenades."

Brakemeyer did not want to kill anyone unnecessarily. Each team member would use Byrna Technologies HD handguns. Powered by CO2 compressed air, the Byrna shoots six .68 caliber kinetic and chemical irritant projectiles. Hitting a target from 60 feet or closer, bursts the ball making a large cloud of powder. The target's breathing and seeing will feel like the attack of an enormous swarm of stinging bees.

Brakemeyer said, "Circling the estate and eliminating the guards enables entry into the building to find and subdue Cena Cascalho. Traps may be set up around the estate and around doors and windows. Be ready. She will be ready to defend herself with a handgun or worse. Using the Byrna on her should be fine. I shall utilize a knock out shot to keep her under during transport."

In the dark where the B Team utilizes night vision and heat signature tactics, the rich gallery owner would not see her assailants. She would be tagged, bagged, and hustled to the Team's getaway SUV. Her home office would be ransacked to recover computers, digital storage devices, and paper files.

The owner of B-Delta Security and his consultant, Colonel Schmidt, knew the possibility existed that Cena Cascalho might booby-trap her office in case all was lost. Brakemeyer gave her advance warning of his attack. Therefore, Clif concealed in his backpack a Portable Explosive Detector based on Ion Mobility Spectrometry (IMS) technology. Outside and inside the mansion the KD-180 explosive detector would sniff the air and alert to chemical signatures like TNT, ammonium nitrate, RDX, and many others. It might give enough advanced warning to save everyone's life.

***

Clif Brakemeyer invited Nick Falkenrath for a trip on his yacht, the Lujon, from Jack London Square to San Pablo Bay, Suisun Bay, and up the San Joáquin River to the confluence of the Mokelumne River and his berth at the Willow Berm Marina.

The weather warmed with light winds from the west. Seagulls flew about squawking their cries of outrage and hunger. The water reflected blue sky with breeze ripples greeting the bow of the Lujon as it pushed against the fresh water flowing toward the Golden Gate.

From the flybridge, Nick sat in the white co-pilot's chair alongside the captain's chair. Clif kept his attention forward always scanning for floating objects that could damage the boat, and channel markers alerting boaters to navigation hazards like sand bars and shallow water.

Ada returned to Casa Falkenrath from the training facility giving Nick a day with Clif. The discussion was all Ada.

"Colonel Schmidt is the smartest, best-trained soldier I've ever worked with," Clif said evenly. "She's even better than Commander Marcs. By the way, how is Shep the Burmese Mountain dog?"

"He's fine," Falkenrath said. "He sniffed out all the shell casings and unexploded ordinance on my property. He is very protective of Ada and me."

Clif turned the Lujon away from the main river to the channel that passed the city of Antioch and became the San Joáquin River. He fell silent for several miles of travel.

"Are you going to tell me why you wanted me to take this trip with you?" Nick asked. "I imagine you want Ada to keep working for you."

"Two things regarding Colonel Schmidt," Clif said. "We have an unsanctioned mission to Brazil. In order to capture the person that's been blowing up and poisoning people, our team needs to create a little mayhem. There will be opposition with help from the Rio de Janeiro police."

"If anything goes wrong you, your team, and Ada will be in a world of hurt. How do you get out of a Brazilian jail?" Nick asked."

"Colonel Schmidt is in charge of our A Team which will raid a private business near Ipanema Beach. Ten minutes and they'll be on their way out of the country. I, on the other hand, lead Team B that must snatch our target in a heavily housed and guarded area thirty minutes away in a community called Joá."

"Jeeze Louise," Nick said. "Ada wants to do this?" Before Brakemeyer could respond Nick said, "Stupid me, of course she does. She isn't afraid of anything. Shit – I mean shoot."

"Believe it or not," Clif said, "I believe the odds are in our favor. We are better trained and equipped than the people we are up against."

"At least they don't know you are coming, right?" Nick said. "The element of surprise is in your favor."

"Actually, Nick, they do know we are coming. They don't know *when*. I've let enough time go by that they may suffer from guard fatigue."

Nick watched the sides of the river turn from flat land to banks holding back floodwaters. He shook his head.

"I don't want to hear anymore," Nick said. "Until you guys return safely, I'm going to be pooping bricks. Do I want to hear the second item you were going to tell me about Ada?"

"B-Delta Security LLC is a very successful business. We have a good and growing client list, although Global International is suffering at the moment. My partner Calvin Chu is taking a break from the work. I need someone to run the company."

"Why?" Nick asked. "Are you going somewhere?"

"I told you about my Swiss girlfriend. Well, I'm going to be a dad."

"And you're moving to Switzerland?" Nick asked incredulously.

"Probably. It's not final yet. If I do, I need to sell this boat and find someone to run B-Delta."

"Can't you operate from Switzerland? You have an international company with clients around the world."

"Possibly," Clif said. "But the client base is strongest in California and the training facilities are in Nevada. I would be a very long-distance manager.

I'd prefer Colonel Schmidt to run the business with me as a consultant."

Nick again shook his head. "Ada and I have pretty good resources but I'm not sure we could afford to purchase B-Delta."

"The fact that you both live in Nevada near the warehouse and training compound is perfect," Clif replied. "The buyout could be over five or ten years and paid for from earnings – and she would still make good money over and above expenses. Colonel Schmidt has all the qualities and capabilities of an international private agent. In addition, you said yourself that she was bored stupid."

"I just don't know if I can support her performing such dangerous work. She'd place herself in the middle of every risky sortie that came along."

"All I ask is that you think about it," Clif said. "Don't mention our conversation until we return from this operation. I will explain my thoughts to her on the return flight home."

"All right," Nick said. "I won't sleep a wink until you guys return. When are you leaving?"

"Day after tomorrow," Clif replied.

"Shit – I mean shoot," Nick said.

Eight
One Man's Mission

From the hospital where Calvin Chu regained consciousness, the explosion victim transferred to St. Mary's Medical Center only two blocks from Beverly Wells' apartment near Golden Gate Park in San Francisco. He underwent CT scans, MRI brain scans, a complete series of neurological, cognitive, and image tests.

After a few days, the doctor released Cal to Beverly as caregiver. She received a complete list of symptoms related to a worsening of his condition such as extreme headaches, nausea, tinnitus, sleeplessness, change of mood, nerve pain, and fainting spells. His memory loss of the incident that caused his concussion was normal, but his sensitivity to light was another symptom of brain trauma.

A member of B-Delta Security brought his SUV to a parking place on Stanyan Street. Cal pulled as much information from the agent as he could – the when, where, and how of the mission to Brazil. Payback for the death of May Tockterman churned in the back of his mind like a dentist's drill on an angry tooth. What the hell good was he if others performed *his obligation* to achieve justice for May? His anger deepened the more he thought about the killer Willie Poe and boss Acucena Cascalho.

Cal fought his concussion symptoms by hiding them. He refused to allow Beverly to examine the pupils of his eyes, question his confusion, fatigue, or blurry vision. Cal attempted to show Beverly gratitude for her caregiver efforts, and act as nice as possible. He insisted on pretending his condition improved daily, rewarding Beverly for her efforts.

A few days later, Cal felt good enough to join his company whether they liked it or not. He rose from bed, swallowed a handful of painkillers, chased them down his throat with bottled water, and dressed for his trip. Beverly Wells left for her office at ARTnews Magazine an hour before, safe in the knowledge that Cal would rest, watch a little TV, and snack from the food items she prepared and stored for him in her refrigerator.

In his overnight backpack, Cal made certain to include his prescription meds, generic meds, and a good book to read like *The Delta Elite* by Del Tritten. A couple bottles of water added to his backpack, plus changes of socks and underwear, and the former detective rushed out the door to his car.

His journey east on Interstate 80 led to Reno and then Fernley, Nevada where he took Highway 95 to the dirt roads leading to the B-Delta Security training compound. When he arrived, the facility resembled a ghost town, as no people were present. Cal parked his SUV and walked into the meeting room where Clif performed all his briefings.

After rummaging through file drawers, desk drawers, maps, and charts, Cal decided to fire up the generator so he could run the computer. He opened the slide show program and bingo!

All the details of the operation were revealed slide after slide. Clif, being the meticulous man that he was, even showed the dates, time, and travel details. The team, dressed as tourists, would arrive at the Reno-Tahoe International Airport at 0:900, board a Gulfstream G650 chartered jet, and fly to Asuncion International Airport in Paraguay. The direct flight would last approximately 12.5 hours.

Cal adjourned to the equipment room where he found an extra team travel bag. He loaded it with tactical clothing from his personal locker, the weapons needed for the assignment, plus disguises. He grabbed large horn-rimmed sunglasses, hat, scarf, and fake mustache from the costume table.

The 20% owner of B-Delta Security walked into the sunshine in direct line with his SUV. He felt confident he'd thought of everything. Even with sunglasses on, the brightness of the high desert almost knocked him over. About ten feet from the vehicle his stomach began to churn and his head started spinning.

Cal collapsed to his knees and threw up. A few minutes passed before recovery brought him back to the world of the uninjured. The nauseous fellow pulled a bottle of water from his backpack and drank the whole thing.

Cal needed tourist clothes to blend in with the team. He drove to a Kohl's store in Reno procuring a tropical shirt covered by a light-tan, island linen coat and matching pants. Dressing in the parking lot outside his SUV, the seriously ill detective drove to the east side of the Reno-Tahoe Airport.

Cal found South Rock Boulevard and drove to a tree-lined parking area across the street from the air charter service. When the team arrived to board the Gulfstream, the unwanted team member would spot them and slip into the group unnoticed – he hoped.

Cal hunkered down in the back seat of his car with a blanket over his head and the doors locked. Sound sleep eluded him but catnaps remained a possibility as he hid from the light an hour before sunset.

His migraines rose and fell like a wave in the deep ocean. Relief from the pain brought the horrible knowledge it would return. Several times during the night, Cal believed in the impossibility of joining the team, but relief from the pain brought hope. Another load of pain pills taken sooner than prescribed brought nausea but also brought relief.

Beverly would likely phone Clif when she realized Mr. Chu vanished from her apartment. Brakemeyer would forge a verbal battle first and then get physical if he had to. Headaches and nausea would limit Cal's ability to force his way on the plane. Sneaking on the plane and remaining unnoticed until it lifted off remained a requirement for success.

Cal awoke to a bright morning sun. Panic swept over him as he realized he had fallen asleep. He checked his cell phone for the time. Thirty minutes until take off meant he needed to get inside the small terminal building for charter flights and hangout until the team arrived, if they hadn't arrived already.

The exhausted detective put on his disguise, grabbed his backpack and gear bag, and walked calmly across the street. He entered the building just in time to see the last team member exit the building toward the jet.

Cal quickened his pace. He looked much like the others with black gear bag and goofy tropical tourist clothes. The team of twelve men, one woman, plus pilot, co-pilot, and one flight attendant meant a full load. Everyone carried their bag onto the plane where the flight attendant stowed them in a luggage compartment resembling an armoire.

As Cal was the last to board, he had to walk down the aisle toward the rear where he intended to lock himself in the plane's lavatory until after takeoff. Each passenger busied him or herself with reading materials, headphones plugged into iPhones, and laptops. Those with window seats stared out their portal as if an alien spacecraft might land any minute.

The stowaway thought he was home free as he reached the last seat. That is when Brakemeyer tapped him on the shoulder. His voice remained low and soft.

"You know we can't depart with you on board my friend. For god's sake, you were almost blown to pieces a few weeks ago. This plane pressurizes to 10,000 feet for almost 12.5 hours. Cal, you're not healed enough from your concussion to survive that kind of travel."

"I can take it," Cal said defiantly.

"What if you can't," Clif said. "You might jeopardize this mission and your own life for no reason."

Brakemeyer thought he could see Cal's eyes burning through his sunglasses with Chinese fury. Cal said, "I have more reason than anyone on this plane and you know it. It will take all of you to drag me off this jet. Hell, you might kill me before we leave the ground. Do you want to risk that possibility?"

"Shit," Brakemeyer said softly. "You are such a stubborn bastard. Did you bring all your meds?"

Cal remained angry. "Of course. How stupid do you think I am?"

"Don't get pissy with me, Chu. You are not only inscrutable and sneaky, but irritable too. Have a seat so we can take off."

As Cal took his seat, Brakemeyer turned to everyone on the plane. He spoke in a shout so he would be heard in the form of an order.

"Listen up team. Despite his concussion, Cal has decided to join our mission. He'll be with me on Team B. I'll have him fully cognizant of operation details long before we reach Asunción in Paraguay."

Cal spoke up. "I already know operation details."

Clif turned to his friend. “Like I said, inscrutable and sneaky.”

***

Acucena Cascalho barked angrily at her security manager, Duarte Eleuterio. He represented her first target of the day. She laced her perfect Brazilian Portuguese with a boatload of foul words.

“Puta merda! (Holy shit) Why will the police not send officers to protect my estate and arrest Sam Lion when he comes to kill me?”

Duarte responded nervously, “The Rio Police Chief says their department is still cleaning up after Carnival. Besides, it has been many weeks since you received the letter. Maybe the Americano changed his plans.”

“*Corno!*” (Fool!) Cena screamed. “*Que porra e essa?* (What the fuck?) I do not care if he doesn’t show up for many months. Sam Lion will come. He will chase me to the ends of the earth. *Merda!* (Shit!) I have donated money to the PCRJ for years, supported every cause, and promised to pay double their usual rate for protection. *Monte de merda* (piece of shit) Chief. How many guards have you added?"

Duarte said, "Six plus our regular staff of six."

"*Nem fodendo!* (No fucking way!) How many private security companies did you contact? I happen to know there are 2,000 of them in Brazil."

The hapless security manager said, "I contacted 20 from on-line websites. Five were no longer in business; twelve said they no longer provide personal guard services, and three said they required indemnity against being sued by your estate if they fail to protect you. Compensation would wipe you out unless you purchased an insurance policy costing five million reais. They claimed all security companies in Brazil require a contract with indemnity clauses and insurance."

"*Desenmerda-te!* (Unshit yourself!) Get on your cell phone and find a security company with lots of men. I don't care about signing an indemnity contract. I'll find an insurance company to provide coverage for private security agents. Now go!"

Cena turned and marched stiff-legged to her office. She plopped into her chair and leaned back, fingers rubbing temples. The sun emerged after a brief morning shower. Outside her window, she could hear the final drops collectively blending on the roof and then falling to their puddles on the ground.

The rich heiress' taste for revenge triggered the wrong reaction from her enemy. Too much time passed since the Defenders of Jasoom, and their goal, ceased to exist. Brakemeyer built a security service of epic international proficiency. The letter to the San Francisco City Police did not produce the effect predicted by her partner.

She still believed the only way to save the earth was population reduction. Climate change functioned as a result of earth's natural cycles along with its accompanying solar activity. Changes were gradual enough for people and nations to cope with it. Human populations, however, continued to expand by the billions. They all needed resources such as food, water, sewer, electricity, and modern conveniences.

Giving her life or death to the cause fell far short of the overall goal of reducing *world* population. The life of Acucena Cascalho was tied to a higher-purpose, a purpose of leadership. The shrink she assaulted once per week for many years called her condition *narcissistic personality disorder* (NPD) coupled with a *superiority complex.* That is why she stopped attending psychiatric sessions. She knew she was far beyond such demeaning babble. Why did the world not see the Cascalho genius? People's lack of vision and understanding packed the world with idiocy. So many human beings filled the planet uselessly. So many human beings placed a horrible burden on those that provided work, shelter, food, and material objects for everyone else.

The only person that functioned at her mental level was Frederick Mahler. His genius, accomplishments, and purpose brought Cena to respect and love the world's most celebrated gallery owner. His murder by Ranjeet Bhabananda left her hollow inside. The Brazilian heiress always felt above men, never needing them for anything other than momentary sexual pleasure. She didn't need Frederick Mahler but *wanted* him in her life, the same way she wanted silk underwear.

Unlike her idiot security guards, not hearing from Brakemeyer meant he planned and practiced for his assault on the Cascalho estate. Cena felt like a goldfish swimming alone in a round fishbowl. Eventually, Sam Lion's catch net would dip in and snag her. Would he kill her outright, torture her, or kill her in a manner fitting of those she had killed?

Defense might prove to be a lifesaver. Cena decided to arm herself to the hilt, and then place a booby-trap where the Americanos least expected it. With Duarte's help, she dressed in tactical body armor, helmet, and jungle boots. She armed herself with two handguns, a 12-gauge shotgun, smoke and frag grenades, three knives, and two Ninja throwing stars.

The booby-traps worked without electricity. Trip wires were set around the perimeter of the property. The guards also set them near doors and windows.

Several trip wires attached to battery-operated sound grenades. When the trip wire activated, the pin pulled out of a small device emitting an ear-piercing 130 dB siren. Other trip wires attached to homemade flash bangs. The trip wire idea meant Cena and the guards would have advanced warning of intruders. She and her guards could concentrate their fire on the unlucky agents falling prey to the booby traps.

The darkness of night gradually removed the color of the day. Streetlights and the lights in homes began winking on. Cena paced around her living room munching on a Coxinhas, (shredded chicken meat with cream cheese,) deep-fried in golden bread-crumbs. She ascended the ultra-modern staircase wrapping around an enormous square granite pillar.

On the second floor, the windows to her right faced the street and the home-covered hills beyond. Cena's driveway and garage lay below her night view. Suddenly, a pair of headlights moved slowly down the street and then turned into her driveway. She expected no one; surely, Sam Lion would not be so bold as to drive up to her front door. The heavily armored Brazilian heiress dropped the plate holding the Coxinhas and rushed down the stairs. With her handgun pulled and ready for action, she threw open her front door and shoved the gun in the face of Horado Vartan, her ex-fiancé.

The stunned artist raised his hands and said, "It's just me; don't shoot."

“What the hell are you doing here?” Cena shouted.

“You have not been to the Galeria in weeks. You promised to promote my next show. Some of my best work is ready for public showing.”

“I’ve got bigger problems than your showing,” Cena barked. “There are men coming to kill me and you shouldn’t be here. I suggest you leave.”

“Cena my love,” Horado said softly, “I will fight for you. You know that. I still love you despite that ugly temper of yours.”

“You’d be ugly tempered too if you watched the planet being destroyed by humans. Forests annihilated, oceans turned into garbage dumps and oil slicks, and animal species dying at unprecedented rates. When you try to do something about it, people try to kill you.”

Horado began to step into the house when Cena stopped him. “Watch your feet. That trip wire an inch from your toes will ruin your day.”

He carefully stepped over the wire and into the house. The artist gazed about the house. He swept his hands in a grand gesture.

"The incredible paintings on the walls of your home testify to the best in human achievement. There is so much to be grateful for, Cena. Ocean garbage is being cleaned up. Forests are being replanted, even in deserts. People and cultures make corrections that improve everyone's lot. Extremism for noble or evil causes always leads to disaster. You know that."

"Easy for you to say," Cena yelled. "No one is trying to kill you."

Horado said, "Let me take you away from here. We can go to Patagonia or Tasmania. The people you say are trying to kill you cannot find you. I promise."

"*Vai tomar no cu!* (Up yours)" Cena turned away from the artist. "Stay or go," Cena said. "It's your funeral."

Vartan could not believe the change in Cena. She resembled a combat ranger with nervous ticks and a killer's psychosis. The woman he knew and fell in love with many years ago, morphed into a demon. Her self-made hell world needed her attention. Time to escape her madness.

Horado slowly retreated to the doorway and forgot about the trip wire. A sudden, loud bang and blinding flash caused him to fall to the ground hoping his eyesight would return to normal, and the ringing in his ears would subside over time. Cena and guards charged the man with guns at the ready.

His dark clothing and flailing gestures led one of the guards to fire into the man. Horado Vartan, successful artist, and former fiancé to Acucena Cascalho lay dead.

Cena holstered her pistol and said, "*Merda!* (Shit!) You idiot. Duarte, call the police and tell them an intruder was accidentally shot. My former fiancé tried to break in and kill me."

The commander of the guards stared in disbelief at his boss. A crocodile possessed more compassion than Cena.

Duarte replied, "Yes boss. I will also redeploy the guards to their posts."

Cena snarled. "And make sure someone resets this trip wire. I'd rather not have Sam Lion sneak through the front door. Why don't we have guard dogs? Get me teams of the nastiest Shepherds you can find."

"Yes boss," the commander of the guards replied. His disgust was palpable. Cena's ego prevented her from seeing it. Horado's fate, although unfortunate, fell below her ability to care. Duarte wondered if he was on the wrong side of this battle.

Nine
The Journey to Joá

Their air route took the B-Delta Security team from Reno, across the Gulf of California, over the Pacific Ocean to a point south of Lima, Peru. They banked across the northern corner of Chile, Bolivia, and then Paraguay.

Colonel Schmidt took over the pilot's duties flying the Gulfstream from the Galapagos Islands to the Tropic of Capricorn, and then a hard bank left across the snow-capped Andes to Paraguay. The team's pilot took over for the landing at Aeropuerto-Asuncion or Asuncion International Airport.

During the long flight, the team members took hourly turns performing calisthenics in the isle of the aircraft – pushups, setups, deep knee bends. Only Calvin Chu remained in a semi-fetal position, port window shade pulled down, sunglasses on, and prescription pain medication in the form of Oxycodone taken every few hours. To quell the nausea, he also took Zofran. Cal polished off a 12 oz. bottle of drinking water every 40 minutes or so.

The B-Delta Gulfstream touched down at Asuncion International at 1:30 a.m. The pilot brought the jet across the end of the runway to a location next to the taxiway and shut it down. The AW139 helicopter sat nearby waiting for the team to transfer. The Defion security company really possessed influence in South America. Paraguay, one of the poorest countries in South America, did not pass up the chance for extra money. The passport officer from the airport jumped off a golf cart he'd ridden from the main terminal. The Defion helicopter pilot, B-Delta's pilot, Brakemeyer, and Colonel Schmidt handed a stack of passports to the man. He resumed his seat in the golf cart. With a flashlight held by Brakemeyer, he quickly stamped all the passports and handed them back.

"A team of scientists here to study the Iguazú Falls," the customs official said.

Colonel Schmidt in her finest Spanish said, "You will find our Customs Declarations in order."

"I am certain they are." He waived off her attempt to hand them over.

He addressed himself to the Defion agent. "Senior Ignacio Quispe, your jet shall refuel here as well as your helicopter when you return. Is that correct?"

"Yes, sir," Igi replied. "Here is our fee for your airport's extra service."

The roll of Nuevo Sol banknotes in 200 denominations disappeared so quickly from the agent's hand it was as if it was never there to begin with. Ignacio finished his dialogue with the corrupt customs official.

"My scientific friends have suffered a very long flight and would like to retire to their hotel for the night. Thank you, officer, for your excellent work. I shall make commendations to your superiors."

The customs official smiled weakly and said, "Please do not praise me too highly or they will know *something is up.* I believe your hotel van is waiting at passenger pick up. It is a very long walk from here. I suggest you and your *scientists* walk that road over there to the Avenue Aviador Silvio Pettirossi. I shall tell your hotel van to pick you up there. The walk will be much shorter."

"Gracias Senior," Ignacio said. Brakemeyer and Ada also said Gracias.

The customs official swung his golf cart around and took off at surprising speed. By the time their bags were transferred to the helicopter and overnight bags collected for the hike to the avenue, the van from the Dazzler by Wyndham Asuncion drove onto the pad near the Gulfstream. The super-friendly driver bowed constantly as he assisted everyone to their seats and placed their backpacks in the luggage compartment at the van's rear. After receiving a generous tip from Ignacio, he drove quickly but carefully to the Dazzler, an ultra-modern, 20-story hotel on the Avenue Aviadores Del Chaco and Vansconcellos.

The hotel's front desk agent welcomed the big group with an affable nod and smile. He looked as tired as the members of the group. Brakemeyer reminded the team just after landing that they were very tired scientists. They should talk and act accordingly.

Everyone received their room keys and retired without incident. Being four time zones later in California and Nevada, the sun rose sooner in Paraguay than the group liked. When they crossed the border into Brazil, they would move back another hour by the clock. The target time to Pedra Bonita peak was 1:00 a.m. The AW139's flight time to Cornélio Procópio of about three hours, half-hour to refuel, and three hours to Pedra Bonita meant they would leave Asuncion at 8:30 p.m.

Everyone besides Brakemeyer and Cal slept in until mid-morning. After 12.5 hours of catnapping and hiding from the light, Cal was unable to sleep. Brakemeyer shared his room with his friend to keep an eye on him. Cal rambled on about the death of May Tockterman, the need for justice, his excellent care by Beverly Wells, and his return to detective work. He didn't even notice when Clif dropped off to sleep. Cal continued talking to the walls, furniture, and window.

By noon, the B-Delta team, except for Cal, ate lunch on the roof in their swimming gear. After lunch and a brief respite, they took turns swimming laps in the rooftop pool with a view. Ada chatted nonsense with her team to keep them from waxing too serious. At 5:00 p.m., they all met in Brakemeyer's King Suite for the final briefing with emphasis on actions needed when things turned to shit. At 6:00 p.m., they ate dinner in quiet certitude. At 7:00 p.m., the van driver loaded the team and then steered the big Ford Transit Wagon to their helicopter.

Ignacio and the Gulfstream pilots arrived by taxi and began preparing the AW139. Igi engaged a lengthy and detailed pre-flight check. Brakemeyer and Colonel Schmidt spoke with their Gulfstream Captain and co-pilot. The team would be back by morning so they needed to stay inside the plane, make certain it remained flight-ready, and prepped for medical emergencies.

While in Reno, Brakemeyer stocked the jet with a half-dozen EMT First Responder Medical Kits. Each kit contained 568 pieces in a large orange bag. Separate bags contained everything from disposable skin staplers to complete I.V. drip administration equipment. A portable heart monitor with blood oxygen saturation and pulse oximeter rounded out the emergency care equipment. Cal and Brakemeyer put each team member through EMT training and certification; they could care for each other in a pinch.

At 8:30 p.m. sharp, Igi received clearance from the control tower to ascend to 10,000 feet as the AW139 flew west toward the border with Brazil. His flight plan filed with the AIS unit found its way via the Internet program Radio COM. It showed the flight ending at Ciudad Del Este, Paraguay.

The ex-military helicopter pilot wound up the big machine and lifted off. Colonel Schmidt sat in the left seat as co-pilot or Lieutenant. His use of two hands and two feet to control the aircraft seemed nothing short of a miracle to Brakemeyer. Colonel Schmidt's ability to fly the craft also struck the B-Delta owner as amazing. The cyclic control stick, collective lever, and foot pedals required perfect coordination to make the aircraft perform correctly without crashing. He envied Nick Falkenrath having landed such a talented and fearless woman of remarkable beauty. He knew bringing her home alive fell into the area of high priority. Managing the problems of his partner Calvin Chu held greater importance. Cal resembled a newly released prisoner from Devil's Island.

The night flight to Cornélio Procópio encountered little in the way of cloud cover. Winds blew light at four miles per hour over mostly flat land interspersed with low hills.

Igi flew a route about five miles north of the town of Cornélio Procópio to minimize their rotor noise over a populated area. He angled across empty agricultural land until he found the southwest end of the airport runway. One dim light lit the fueling area where one man, responsible for airport maintenance, waited with a fuel truck manufactured just after World War II.

Ignacio settled the big chopper on the pavement marked with a circle and X. As soon as the rotorblades slowed to a stop, the pilot climbed from his seat and approached the maintenance man. They spoke rapid fire Spanish.

Brakemeyer and Ada watched through the darkness into the weak, orange light of the tiny terminal building. They watched Ignacio walk to the fueling truck and immediately begin yelling at the hapless maintenance man. He marched back to his AW139 and spoke to Brakemeyer through the open door.

"This idiot brought us a tanker filled with Avgas instead of jet fuel. I clearly told his boss at Petrobras to send a tanker full of jet fuel. Avgas is meant for piston engines and jet fuel is meant for turbines. These are twin turbines generating 1,531 horsepower. I can't use rusty Avgas from an old beater tanker truck from World War II."

Brakemeyer asked, "How many miles can we fly on the fuel you have remaining?"

Ignacio and Ada answered simultaneously. "Two hundred and fifty."

"That takes care of that option," Clif said. "After ordering another tanker with jet fuel this time, how long before it gets here?"

Ignacio fumed in fury as he thought. Finally, he said, "My best guess is jet fuel will need to come from the Curitiba airport facility - a five or six hour drive after they load the truck and send it on its way."

Brakemeyer looked at Colonel Schmidt. "Any ideas?" he asked.

Ada said, “We have no choice but to hide out in one of the empty hangers here until the fuel truck arrives. We refuel and wait until this time tomorrow night, and then resume our undertaking.”

Brakemeyer lowered his voice so only Colonel Schmidt could hear. “Every day Cal is not under the care of a doctor in a hospital, he’s at great risk of a breakdown or death. I don’t like the option . . . but I guess there is no other way.”

“We are definitely stuck here in Brazil in the middle of nowhere,” Ada said. “I recommend Ignacio and his brethren at Defion make the calls and bribes necessary to get our fuel here as fast as possible.”

Brakemeyer breathed a heavy sigh. “Agreed.” He turned to Igi and said, “I’ve got the monetary backing to complete this operation. If you and Defion will trust me, please carry the burden of bribing and paying for the fuel we need as fast as *Brazilian possible.*”

Despite his anger boiling over, Ignacio smiled and said, “You just proclaimed the magic words my friend.”

Ignacio pulled his cell phone and tapped a number for his home office. Brakemeyer and team waited in the helicopter. Igi finished his phone call, and then stood two inches from the maintenance man. He barked in the man's face leaving no room for doubt about his obligation to hide the people in the helicopter.

Shaking fearfully, the man pointed at a hanger about 200 feet from Ignacio's aircraft. It was the first building constructed at right angles to a row of four hangers parallel to the runway. It sat in the perfect position to allow observation of the helicopter and anyone approaching the tiny terminal house parking area. Bushy green trees surrounded the maintenance man's small one bedroom house directly across from the hanger and in line with the tiny terminal.

Ignacio approached the door of the chopper and spoke to Brakemeyer. "Delmo here says we can stretch out and rest in that empty hanger over there. He expects no aircraft to use the field until the week-end. Bring all you need to sleep and wait out the hours."

“How long until the fueling truck arrives?” Clif asked.

“It will be loaded with jet fuel and depart Curitiba at 7:30 tomorrow morning. Baring accidents it will arrive after lunch time, about 1:30 p.m.”

Brakemeyer said, “We need to pull this chopper into the hanger and out of sight. We’ll use the ropes we brought along to lash to the cockpit step loops. We’ll tie knots in the ropes so the entire team can get a hand hold and pull this bad boy into the hanger.”

Colonel Schmidt said to Ignacio, “Ask Delmo for a lantern of some kind, and arrange for a big pot of Feijoada for breakfast and lunch.”

“So, you like black bean stew with pork and a side of rice?” Igi teased.

“Or bread,” Colonel Schmidt said.

“Our stew in Lima is much better,” Igi boasted. “I will advise Delmo of our needs. If he does not have enough food in his house to feed us, I will go into town with him and purchase what we need. Let’s go settle in for the night.”

***

Domestic violence in Brazil, as everywhere else in the world, seemed an epidemic of male vs. female. Much to her displeasure, Acucena Cascalho found herself removed from her home and driven in a police van to the Ipanema Police Station. Her interrogation by stern-faced police detectives, left little doubt of her non-standing with the PCRJ. The private guard that shot and killed Horado Vartan also found himself in custody.

Cena's stories concerning her ex-fiancé trying to kill her appeared suspicious. A tall tale of a group of American assassins trying to kill her appeared an excuse to cover her private guard shooting an un-armed man. All she could tell them was the name Brakemeyer and Chu, and B-Delta Security.

The question the police kept asking was *what did she do* to have North American assassins trying to kill her? She refused to divulge her foreign affairs. She remained an important citizen of Brazil and the world art community. She maintained her erudite, highbrow attitude as though they had arrested the president of Brazil.

The background check on Horado Vartan showed a model citizen, and artist of some renown. His criminal record amounted to three parking tickets in five years. A background check on Acucena Cascalho found a Brazilian aristocrat with inquiries from the American FBI and San Francisco City Police Department over two years ago. She was a person of interest in an investigation into the murder of Frederick Mahler and a strange, illegal entomological operation. Very, very strange and suspicious.

After hours of cross-examination, Cena's attorney, drug from his bed, arrived and defended his client against all inferences and accusations. He achieved her release and drove her home. The police left Cena with a stern warning that there had better not be any further violence at her home. Her status as socialite would not protect her. She assured the police that her friends high up in government would not protect them if anything happened to her.

***

Sitting in pressurized aircraft for hours on end made the B-Delta team grateful for the aircraft hangar with the room to pace, run around, and stretch out and sleep. Watch duty changed every two hours as someone kept an eye on the surrounding area. Weapons remained ready.

At sunrise, Calvin Chu paced about the hanger holding his head and muttering to himself. He approached Brakemeyer and asked a serious question.

"Where are we Clif?"

Brakemeyer's answer qualified as flippant. "I've been asking myself that same question. We are in an airplane hangar a few miles outside of Cornélio Procópio, Brazil. We are waiting for jet fuel to arrive from Curitiba. How are you feeling my friend? You look like shit."

Cal asked, "Are we going after Acucena Cascalho?"

Clif sighed and said, "There is no other reason for us to enter Brazil illegally, kidnap one of their important citizens, and extract her and her electronic data."

The two men sat on the cold concrete with their backs to the hanger door. Clif began an interrogation of the man to determine how bad his concussion symptoms really were.

"Cal, you must answer truthfully yes or no to my questions. Lying will not help me help you. You have a concussion that did not have time to heal. Are we in agreement?"

"Okay, but you will not remove me from this mission."

"Do you have headaches?

"Yes, that's why I am taking the Oxycodone and Zofran."

"Ringing in the ears? Nausea? Vomiting?"

"Ringing yes, nausea and vomiting not since before we left Reno."

"Blurry vision or seeing stars?"

"Yes, occasionally."

"You are sensitive to light and noises and you don't sleep. I already know that."

"I can't taste or smell anything either."

Cal decided to stand up. He wobbled slightly, and then crumbled to the floor. He began twitching and jerking.

Brakemeyer yelled, "Johnson, bring me a medical bag fast! Cal is having a seizure."

Clif rolled Cal onto his side and placed a rolled blanket under his head. Ada took video of Cal's condition with her cell phone. His body calmed after about two minutes. Clif pulled a thermometer from the medical bag and took Cal's temperature.

"He's two points high," Brakemeyer said. "Let's make a cold compress for his forehead."

Another minute rolled by. The damaged detective opened his eyes and slowly pushed himself to a sitting position.

"What happened?" Cal croaked.

"You just experienced a seizure, my friend," Clif replied.

"No way," Cal said with some anger. "I've never had a seizure in my life."

"You've never been blown half way across a marina into a palm tree either. You have a severe concussion Cal. You might end up with permanent brain damage, slurred speech, dizziness, and confusion. You must stay here with Delmo the airfield maintenance man. He can take care of you until we return from Joá to refuel for the flight back to Asuncion."

Cal began to cry. Tears streaked his face as he spoke in choking sobs.

"You dirty . . . bastard. You rotten son of a bitch. I'll hate you for the rest of my life. We will never be friends again if you don't allow me to help catch Cascalho. I owe her for what happened to May and the others."

Brakemeyer reached his limit with his partner's stubborn, irrational attitude. He said, "I will sacrifice our friendship to keep you alive. Without hospital care, you will be crippled mentally and physically for life. Supporting your need for vengeance is irresponsible on my part. I am here to see that Cena pays for her deeds and you live undamaged through this concussion."

"Fucker!" Cal attempted a shout but dizziness overcame him.

Brakemeyer waited until Cal could understand his words. Clif said, "I'll make you a deal, Chu. Are you listening?"

"Fucker," Cal said with less enthusiasm.

"If you will rest here and recover for the trip home, we will bring Acucena Cascalho to you – right here. You and she may have a private talk for as long as you like. Well?"

"Turncoat, traitor, Judas," Cal growled.

"You left out Benedict Arnold, back-stabber, and apostate," Brakemeyer said smiling.

The leader of B-Delta Security spoke to Ignacio about Cal's condition. The Defion agent left the hangar and found Delmo in his house. The maintenance man offered his bed for Cal to rest in. It's comfort far exceeded the concrete floor of the hangar.

Brakemeyer pulled Cal's left arm around his shoulder and Colonel Schmidt bent his right arm around her shoulder. Sunglasses on, they helped Cal walk slowly to Delmo's home and his surprisingly comfortable bed. The detective fell asleep the moment his head hit the pillow.

Ignacio via Brakemeyer spoke in detailed Spanish how to administer Cal's meds, food, and water. He also instructed him on what to do if the American acted strangely, experienced another seizure, or tried to leave the house before the team returned. Ignacio assured Delmo the team would return by 8:00 a.m. tomorrow morning.

Ten

Retribution and Justice

The jet fuel tanker arrived at 1:20 p.m. With beaker in hand, Ignacio drew multiple samples from the tank making certain it didn't harbor particulates of any kind. The tanker driver backed the rig up to the hanger. The door rolled slowly on its rails until enough space existed to drag the fuel hose to the AW139's aft fueling port. They topped off the fuel system, and then drove the tanker to Delmo's workshop building. Enough room existed to hide the truck until the team returned to refill the chopper's 414-gallon fuel tank.

Until their departure time at 7:00 p.m., everyone performed calisthenics. They also reviewed road maps with their route from Taubaté to Joá and their two targets marked in red. Equipment and weapon checks finished the afternoon. For dinner, they enjoyed the delicious black bean soup prepared by Delmo and Ignacio. Colonel Schmidt especially enjoyed the Pão de Queijo or Brazilian cheese bread.

Departure time arrived with every member of the team anxious to get going and get the job done. The AW139 was pulled and pushed from the hanger to the airstrip.

The darkness of night overtook sunset as they lifted off for their two-hour flight to Taubaté. The weather forecast included patchy clouds, temperatures in the high 60's, and light winds. Ignacio and Colonel Schmidt wore night vision goggles attached to their helmets. Igi activated their TAWS or terrain awareness warning system with vertical guidance. Because night vision goggles made depth perception tricky at best, when they reached Taubaté farm, Colonel Schmidt called out the vertical distance to ground as Igi lowered the chopper to a soft landing.

Two Toyota 4Runners waited for them at the edge of the field, one dark burgundy and one black. Even though the vehicles contained just enough fuel and mileage to make a round trip to Joá, each SUV held a five-gallon jerry can of unleaded gas strapped to the rear luggage area. This turned out to be a thoughtful inclusion by the Defion planners.

Ada ran to the black 4Runner while Brakemeyer ran to the dark Burgundy 4Runner. They fired up their vehicles and drove them to the chopper to load their equipment and weapons. They performed mic checks on their radios, piled the teams into their respective vehicles, and wheeled east on Road 139 Rodovia Doutor Caio Gomes Figuerirado.

They reached the town of Pindamonhangaba to connect with BR116 Rodovia Presidente Dutra. Two hours later, they reached the heavily populated regions outside Rio de Janeiro. A confusing tangle of highways, streets, and avenues brought them to their rendezvous at Estrada do Joá and Rua Jackson de Figueiredo.

Colonel Schmidt checked her paper map against the '*to and from*' Google map on her 4Runner's computer display screen. A quick confab with Brakemeyer and Team A left the rendezvous to negotiate the Estrada do Joá leading to Ipanema.

Brakemeyer and Team B waited patiently and quietly for thirty minutes before driving a third of a mile to Acucena Cascalho's home on the Rua Jackson de Figueiredo loop.

***

Heavy stands of trees lined the Rua Anibal Mendonça. Across from the Cascalho Galeria, Colonel Schmidt parked the black SUV.

Streetlights from the Avenue Vieira Souto, running parallel to Ipanema Beach, cast more light on the Galeria Building than the team liked. Dozens of adjoining hotels faced the beach with room lights also illuminating the area. The Galeria sat on the edge of a very bright mile.

Johnson stayed behind and hid in a dark doorway near the car. Colonel Schmidt and the rest of the team, dark clothing and hoods in place, crept across the street and down the alley next to the Galeria. Long ago, electricians mounted the breaker box outside and mid-way between the front and back. A long pipe carried the wires to the attic where they dispersed down through the walls to all the rooms.

They were about to throw the main breaker to *off* when Johnson whispered into his radio mic, "Colonel, we have a problem."

A city police car cruising slowly down the street, slowed at the SUV. The two officers saw something they thought suspicious and pulled behind the car and stopped.

Ada whispered to Johnson, "Neutralize them before they can look up license plate numbers. You've got two minutes."

With cool dispatch, Johnson pulled his Byrna handgun. From the shadows, he waited until the two officers left their vehicle and began searching around the SUV with flashlights.

When they both stood on Johnson's side of the car, one officer shining a light in the back window and one in the front, Johnson said, "Hello gentlemen."

The two policemen turned toward the sound and swung their flashlights to see the person speaking English. Two pop-pops and the men fell to the ground coughing and gagging. Johnson ran to them and zip-tied their hands and feet. He dragged them to their police car and shoved them inside.

The A Team second-in-command whispered into his microphone, "Problem solved Colonel. Make it quick. We need to get out of here."

Ada replied, "Roger that."

The breaker box opened with the touch of a small crow bar. All breaker switches were thrown including the main. The outside lights immediately darkened. The team split into two groups. One sprinted for the front door, while the other for the back. With the alarm system down, they broke through the doors with ease.

Night vision goggles allowed them to quickly dash through the gallery searching for computer laptops, and files. The first team through the front remained on the lower floor while the second team sprinted upstairs to the second floor.

Colonel Schmidt put out a hand to stop the team on the stairs. She witnessed a flashlight beam scanning the hallway above them. An overweight night watchman jingled and creaked down the hall. The noise from his excessive load of gun, ammo belt, whistle, and mic cord almost drowned out his radio calls for help.

Ada waved up one of her team to neutralize the man. He shot the guard in the chest bursting the chemical ball. The man began coughing and throwing up. In moments, his hands and feet met the same fate as the officers outside. Colonel Schmidt waved her men to check the offices along the hall. Quick as cats, they plundered the rooms and re-entered the hall empty handed.

Ada hit the jackpot in the room at the end of the hall facing the street. She handed Cena's laptop to one of her team, and then signaled everyone to open file and desk drawers. They grabbed all the files and stuffed them in a large, black duffel. Ada clutched at the desk drawer and recovered several thumb drives and CD's. They also found the bottom of the duffel bag.

Colonel Schmidt heard the beep from her wristwatch alarm. "It's time to go. Johnson, start the car."

All the agents scrambled out the front door of the Galeria and ran for the 4Runner. Advancing sirens could be heard in the distance.

The Colonel said, "Somebody raised the alarm. We can't use our escape route since it takes us toward the sirens. Hang a right on the Avenue Vieira Souto and then turn when I tell you."

Johnson drove as directed. Ada scanned her map and then scanned the signs and exits that took them to the Estrada Lagoa Barra freeway. She almost missed the exit for Estrada do Joá, but Johnson's quick reaction swerved their SUV just before the concrete divider. He couldn't straighten out in time to make the off-ramp loop so he four-wheeled across the grass slope to Estrada do Joá. After the bouncing subsided and they turned left, the thirty minutes to their rendezvous meant they were in the clear.

***

Brakemeyer and Team B found the power pole closest to Cena's home. One of the agents fired a special gun similar to the one casting the net that caught Willy Poe. This one, however, shot a copper wire net connected to the gun like a Taser. The voltage performed a melting of the wire connecting the transformer's high voltage bushing to the high voltage surge arrester.

Sparks flew in several directions sending the top of the hill, and its million-dollar homes, back to the Stone Age. They drove a few hundred yards with headlights off utilizing their night vision goggles. The six men plus Brakemeyer climbed the hill from the road to Cena's swimming pool.

They knew with the power off, Cena and her neighbors would be using her cell phone to alert the police and power company. The guards ranging the property delineated the areas where trip wires might be hiding.

Team B quickly dispatched four guards with the chemical pellets from their Byrna handguns. Five of the men found trip wires and stepped over them. One did not. He triggered an insidious scream from a noise making devise. The sound dropped him to his knees with hands over his ears. Brakemeyer ran to his position and stomped on the devise with his heel. It stopped shrieking.

The devise brought the remaining outside guards firing their 9mm handguns and a deadly .308

rifle. Brakemeyer dove for cover behind a tree as his men, spread wide across the property, opened up on the guards. All eight fell to the ground with spasms of choking agony.

Brakemeyer spoke to his mic and said, "Advance on the house. Watch for traps at the doors and windows."

Inside the mansion, Cena hid in an upper room with six guards staged around her while six others waited behind furniture on the ground floor. She clutched her handgun, trembling as she and her protectors heard the ruckus outside.

Three of the dark figures from Team B fired smoke grenades through windows on three sides of the home. The guards were ill prepared for an assault of this nature. They ran for the doors to breath fresh air and tripped their own booby traps. The flash bangs blinded everyone for a moment. Team B recovered first and struck the stumbling men with chemical balls as they exited the house.

From their backpacks, Team B slipped on their full face, tactical gas masks. They repositioned their helmets and night vision goggles and ran to the doors where the trip wires no longer represented a threat. Expecting live fire from guards on the inside, the team met no opposition.

Brakemeyer said, “Quick sweep of the first floor then up the stairs. Our target will likely be hiding up there with guards for protection. Gas ‘em.”

The team advanced to the top of the stairs and fired more exploding gas canisters in all directions. The entire second floor became a fog bank of white smoke. No sounds of distress met their ears. The double doors leading to the master suite at the end of the hall appeared to be the logical place their target hid out.

Brakemeyer swung a door-breaching ram at the locked handle. The double doors flew open triggering gunfire from the guards surrounding Cena. Two gas canisters were launched into the room. The trapped people inside bolted for the sliding glass door leading to the balcony. They found themselves pelted with chemical balls making their world even worse after their gassing.

Brakemeyer spotted the only woman in the group covered in tactical, combat gear. He tackled her and attempted to subdue the Brazilian heiress. Coughing and crying she fought like a wildcat. Her strength surprised the B-Delta owner as he found himself stabbed repeatedly by a knife she'd extracted from her boot. His protective vest prevented life-threatening wounds to his vital organs, but she managed to cut and stab his left arm and leg.

The opportunity for a solid right cross to Cena's jaw presented itself. Brakemeyer, with adrenalin surging, plowed his fist into her face. The blow stopped her crazed battle for life. He hit her a second and third time smashing her nose, and sending her into unconsciousness.

While the team zip tied Cena's guards, Brakemeyer in his distress rolled the demented woman on her stomach and zip tied her hands behind her back. He tied her feet and then spoke to his men via radio.

"I'm hurt. I need someone to pack our target to the car. Let's evac now."

Men rushed to his aid. One of them hoisted the sturdy woman over his shoulder and quick-timed out of the house. Brakemeyer threw his good arm around the shoulder of one of his men and limped out of the house, passed the swimming pool, and down the hill to the waiting SUV.

As they piled into the car, sirens could be heard in the direction of their rendezvous location. Brakemeyer winced with each move of his arm and leg.

"Drive toward the sirens," he said. "Maybe we can slip through. If not, we'll have to fight our way out."

The team drove toward their rendezvous with weapons ready. Cena lay on her side in the back of the SUV, tied, gagged, and still unconscious. As they approached the nexus of Estrada do Joá and Rua Jackson de Figueiredo, the sirens fell silent. They arrived to find the police car blocked by Team A's SUV. The officers lay on the ground, wrapped up by the lines fired from multiple BolaWrap guns. The lights and siren from the police car were turned off.

Colonel Schmidt stuck her face in the driver's side window. "Where is Commander Brakemeyer?"

From the back seat Brakemeyer said, "I got stung by the Brazilian gallery wasp. I'm ok. Thanks for the help with police. Let's get going, and don't break any traffic laws."

Ada said, “Roger that. Follow us.”

***

Calvin Chu’s anger slowly morphed into despair. He rested on Delmo’s bed with his left arm resting on his forehead.

Delmo walked in and said, “Como você está se sentindo esta manhã?”

Cal turned his head to examine the nice but slightly eccentric maintenance man. He did not understand a word Delmo uttered.

“No, I’m not hungry,” Cal said. “Ignacio and Americanos arrive yet?”

Delmo understood his question. “Não senhor.” He looked at his wristwatch and then motioned to Cal.

“Quatro horas para ir.” He held up four fingers and then pointed at his watch. “Eles chegarão em quatro horas.”

Cal said, “Yeah, yeah. I understand four hours - if they are coming back in four hours. They’ll probably land in a Brazilian jail and I'll be stuck here. I need a gun so I can blow my brains out."

Delmo sighed. He knew Cal's condition brought the man pain and depression.

He said, "Seus amigos vão voltar."

Cal replied, "Whatever. I need to go for a walk."

Headache subsiding meant the detective could slowly pull himself out of bed and stand upright. He wobbled causing Delmo to move to support him.

"I'm fine," Cal said.

He stepped carefully from the bedroom. Cal remembered to slip on his B-Delta ball cap and ultra-dark sunglasses before venturing outside.

The day offered blue skies with large puffy clouds slowly drifting in front of the sun and away again. Cal attempted to focus his thoughts on the B-Delta operation as he walked. The sun's brightness caused the light sensitive concussion victim to pull down his ball cap's brim throwing shade on his face.

The dirt road between the crops planted on large rectangles ran arrow-straight for almost a mile. Cal walked the distance before the road angled right and ran another straight mile. He walked until he could see at least five farmhouses surrounded by trees, outbuildings, tanks, and farm equipment.

That is when he heard the shotgun blast and a man riding an ATV barreling at him full speed. Cal threw his arms in the air in surrender. The angry farmer jumped from his Yamaha ATV four-wheeler while keeping his shotgun aimed squarely at Cal's chest.

He screamed at the trespasser demanding to know all kinds of information Cal did not possess or understand. An old beater pickup tossed a cloud of dirt skyward as it raced down the dirt road from the airfield. Delmo slid the truck to a stop directly behind his guest. A cloud of red dust enveloped all three men.

"Delmo," the farmer said in rapid fire Portuguese. "You know this Chinese man? He looks like a spy for China or a terrorist."

Delmo became livid dealing with the man's ignorance and stupidity. "He is an American from San Francisco. He flew in with a team of scientists but got sick along the way. They stopped at my field and asked me to care for him until they returned. Now back off for god's sake."

A faint whapping noise slowly grew louder as the men stopped shouting long enough to watch a helicopter approach the airfield from the east.

"Seus amigos estão aqui," Delmo said excitedly.

The airfield maintenance man scolded the farmer with one last burst of Portuguese profanity. He motioned for Cal to get in the truck. The two men drove to a dirt field access road where they circled and drove back to the airfield.

Cal's heart leaped as he saw his friend and B-Delta team exit the chopper. Ignacio motioned at Delmo to bring the tanker fuel truck. They would re-fuel and take off immediately for Asuncion Paraguay.

Cal felt so elated at seeing his companions he temporarily forgot about Cena Cascalho. He then spotted her being pulled from the helicopter by Colonel Schmidt. An agent threw her over his shoulder and headed for the big hangar.

Cal approached the team and said, "Where's Brakemeyer?"

"I'm here," the bandaged fighter said. "That is one of the nastiest people I've ever had to deal with. I should have asked Colonel Schmidt to take her captive."

Cal said, "You promised you'd bring her to me and you did. Thank you Clif."

"Are you going to take back all those foul things you said about me?"

"Yes, of course," Cal replied. "I guess I should have some alone time with Ms. Cascalho."

Clif said, "You've got as long as it takes to fuel the chopper."

The gagged and tied Cena lay on the cold concrete of the hangar. She regained consciousness on the flight from Taubaté farm. Her fear brought images of being tossed out the helicopter door. When that failed to happen, she somehow knew this small airfield in the middle of nowhere Brazil, remained her last hope of survival.

She pleaded with Cal through her gag. He removed the speech impediment and pulled her to a sitting position.

"Please untie me. My hands and feet are numb. Please."

Cal walked to the nearby corner of the hanger and grabbed an old wooden chair. He plunked it down in front of Cena with its back facing her. He sat down a few feet from her and crossed his arms across the back of the chair.

"You and I have never met Ms. Cascalho. My name is Calvin Chu, former Detective Calvin Chu of the San Francisco City Police Department."

"Please cut my ties, please," Cena whined.

Cal stood up from the chair. He shouted at his captive, "You will shut the hell up until I am done talking. Thank you."

He sat once again and began his dialogue. "Your friends with the Defenders of Jasoom stripped me naked and dumped me in a trailer full of deadly insects. I watched Julia Delmar die a horrible death as the insects swarmed her and feasted on her. You sent killers after Clif Brakemeyer, Beverly Wells, and several other important art people. You managed Willie Poe as he killed people and blew up cargo containers and retail stores. You blew up my boat and killed my fiancé and almost killed me. You have zero reason to go on living. Justice must be served."

Cena began to pee her pants as she recognized the cold-blooded killer behind Calvin Chu's eyes. She whimpered, "Please no. Don't hurt me, please. I'll tell you anything you want if you'll let me go."

Cal reached out and slapped her face with considerable force. "I said shut the hell up!"

Brakemeyer banged on the closed hangar door and yelled, "Ten minutes Chu. You've got ten minutes."

"He means you've got ten minutes," Cal said to Cena. "I will consider your offer of information in exchange for your life. Tell me who your boss or partner is. Who came up with the crazy Sloughhouse type trick and letters?"

Cena almost shouted, "It was Gordon Wicks. He had the idea for the letters and methods to dispose of the people that ruined the mission of the Defenders of Jasoom."

Cal felt disbelief. He asked, "Gordon Wicks? Really? He is in prison. What connection was he to the Defenders of Jasoom?"

"Wicks was the founder of our group. He wanted to steel art and pocket the money. Frederick Mahler saw the group and its activities as a means of funding his idea to reduce world populations. Eventually, Frederick took over the group and its mission. Wicks thought he'd never get caught, but Sam Lion, I mean Clifton Brakemeyer caught him and put him in jail. He wanted payback for what Brakemeyer did to him. Is that enough? Will you let me go?"

Cal replied, "Yes, Ms. Cascalho, I'll let you go. First we must take you somewhere in the helicopter."

He stood and re-fixed the gag in Cena's mouth. She shook her head violently as he lifted her over his shoulder and struggled to get her out of the hanger and into the helicopter. He tied her in the first seat next to the sliding door. Cal pulled the heavy door breaching ram and tied it between her legs. Cena knew her enemy's intention. She thrashed with all her might to no effect.

After Cal spoke with Brakemeyer and Ignacio their course was set. Ignacio stuffed a wad of cash in Delmo's hand – more money than he would have made in a year of farming and maintaining the airfield. He bowed and wished them well.

The AW139 lifted off with Igi in the pilot's seat and Colonel Schmidt in the co-pilot's seat. They angled slightly northwest toward the dam of the Represa Porto Primavera reservoir. When they neared the lake, the agent sitting behind Cena reached forward and pulled the door open. The blast of wind sent Cena into near insanity. Her beauty, position, wealth, and leadership must continue she thought. This couldn't be the end.

A few miles behind the dam in the lakes deepest area, Igi hovered briefly while Cal untied Cena from her seat. He then pulled a revolver from the black bag beneath his feet.

He said to Brazilian Heiress, "This is for May."

Cal shot Cena through the head, and then kicked her body out the door. After a hundred-foot drop, her body hit the water and sank. The weight tied to her feet took her 120 feet to the muddy bottom.

Ignacio lifted the chopper and put on maximum speed to Asuncion. Cal remained quiet, lost in his thoughts. The other members of the B-Delta team felt relief the operation ended successfully. Brakemeyer was a bit worse for wear but justice had been served.

Epilogue

Clifton Brakemeyer accompanied his outdoor groundskeeper Louis to the horse stalls. Clif instructed him on keeping the stalls dry, and daily cleaning of manure and wet straw. Louis' routine involved making certain the barn fans ran in ten-minute cycles and fly traps stayed fresh. Clif even insisted on flysheets, boots, and masks for both horses. A daily grooming with topical sprays composed of pyrethrums and citronella oils rounded out horse care for the new farm hand.

Clif's cell phone rang with the phone address of Calvin Chu. "Hey Cal, what's up? How's Beverly?"

Cal replied, "I am much improved thank you very much. Beverly is fine and still doing the caregiver thing."

"Somebody needs to," Clif said.

"Tell me about your new house. Have you moved in yet?"

"We moved in about two weeks ago. I'll send you photos later today. It is a ranch on ten acres in the Promasens Other Fribourg, Switzerland. You've never seen anything so beautiful. The main house dates back to 1800. It has four bedrooms, eight baths, 3,875 square feet. There's a two-car garage with overhead apartment, horse stalls for four horses, large garden, indoor swimming pool, and a golf course."

"You are shitting me - a golf course?"

"Nine tees and four greens are all beautifully manicured."

"Where is Promasens as it relates to Switzerland the country?"

"Promasens is a small village in a gorgeous valley about half way between Lac Leman and Lac de Neuchâtel. Lausanne, Vevey, and Montreux are only 30 minutes by car in good weather."

"Sounds like you are in the French speaking part of the country."

"Oui, oui Monsieur."

"And how is the Gab-Meister?"

"She and the baby are happy, happy, happy. Her last sonogram indicated a boy is on the way. Her mother and father already visit too much, but that's okay. Gabby is a worker, my god. She's repainting and repairing all over the place. We're surrounded by ag land. I love hearing the tractors plowing and mowing. This place is heaven."

"Married and retired life suites you, my friend."

"What retired? I've got skiing nearby in the winter, golf, fishing, gardening, and horseback riding in the summer. I just hired a farm hand named Louis to cover outdoor landscaping and horse care. Gabby is interviewing for an indoor housekeeper and part-time cook."

"Can't be cheap."

"Selling the Lujon covered our Swiss ranch dollar for Swiss dollar. After cashing in my share of the Willie Poe, Cena Cascalho bit coin fortune, I will have enough Swiss Francs to last forever."

"Every member of the team appreciated the windfall you gave us – in Cayman bank accounts of course."

"Of course."

"By the way, I just learned that Gordon Wicks hung himself in prison. Did you hear about that?"

"I have no response to that. I think the Russians did it. Speaking of B-Delta Security, how is Colonel Schmidt managing the company?"

"I spoke with Blevins the other day. His adjustment to web sales is taking hold. He'll do better than he did with all the retail stores. He's keeping the ones not blown up. The others he shut down. Blevins thinks Colonel Schmidt is the best private investigator and CEO of an international security company he's ever met. No offense."

"None taken. She's the best I've ever encountered including myself."

"So, you have no comment on Wicks hanging himself? A second Sloughhouse letter was found next to his dangling corpse."

"I have no response to that other than saying he got what he deserved. What do you plan to do when the doctors give you the *all clear?*"

"You did say you had an apartment over the garage. I thought I might come visit you."

"Please do. Gabby would love to help you gang up on me. Stay as long as you like. Hell, bring Beverly if you can. You're both welcome."

"Okay my friend. Please book our room. I don't want to lose it to a relative."

"Consider it done."

THE END

www.ingramcontent.com/pod-product-compliance
Lightning Source LLC
LaVergne TN
LVHW050535160826
845677LV00011B/2037

* 9 7 9 8 5 0 9 5 4 2 4 5 9 *